A Thousand Kisses

A Thousand Kisses

Frederic Raphael

www.hhousebooks.com

Hardback ISBN: 978-1-910688-85-4

Cover design by Ken Dawson, Creative Covers
Typeset by Polgarus Studio

Published in the UK

Holland House Books
Holland House
47 Greenham Road
Newbury, Berkshire RG14 7HY
United Kingdom

www.hhousebooks.com

For Peter and Carin Green

In memoriam, Kenneth McLeish

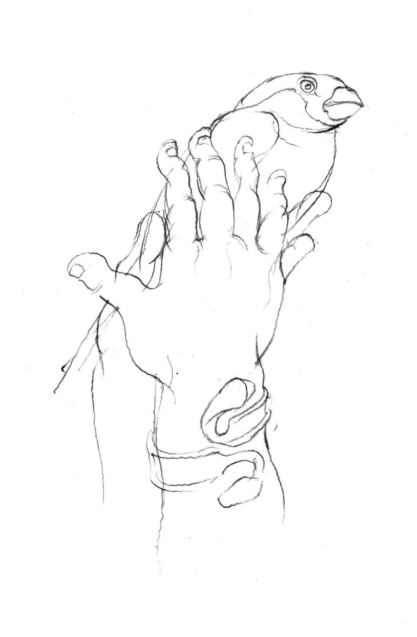

"I hate and I love. You may wonder why I do that."

Gaius Valerius Catullus took the toga of manhood when he was fourteen. Slave girls sized him up. Bought eyes made free with him. Syrian Eirene slides him a glance, guesses secret heat, goes on by, promise and threat, Anatolian smiler. Young pouty-puss they call him, she and Melissa, dark-eyed honey-pot, vernal daughter of a house-slave mother, father whoever it was, Catullus père perhaps, quondam free ranger. Slaves, boys or girls, save busy seducers time. Melissa, Eirene, or some other whisper-footed girl, who will initiate the master's son? He chooses not to know who does the choosing. Female slaves make beds and bets. They guess who and when and where, better than he does; and how.

We were tutored, my brother Manlius and I, by an old Greek slave, fifty-five at least, Solon; sun-shrivelled olive his face, forever wincing – eyes up, brows down – at our northern skies. Exiled Sicilian, when he had us construe Theocritus, "Begin, dear Muses, the bucolic songs, begin; / This is Thyrsis…from Etna…the sweet voice of Thyrsis", he called the poet "*My* Theocritus" and had to blink. His possessive hugged the rustic piper who quit Syracuse's proud tyranny for flat Alexandria, there to play urban shepherd, flyting with flocks of words. Nostalgia collapsed the centuries. Poets, our rarely humourless scholar scowler told us, had no need, if they were good (and only very good was good enough), to pitch themselves into Etna's hot mouth, as Empedocles of steep Agrigento did, doctor, dreamer, dupe, dying to become immortal. Love and hate pumped the ribs of his restless world.

In our Sirmio compound, Lake Garda cuffing either flank, we were all but insulated from vagrant Cisalpine Gauls whose territory Sulla's veterans, and Marius's, had been allotted or grabbed. Father bought out lazy legionaries, took their takings for more than they ever imagined. "Paying over the odds today is tomorrow's bargain," he told us. Solonaki had been knocked down to him in Catanian Naxos; one of a mixed lot, Greeks and barbarians; muscle and meat he had sold on, in Capua, to be gladiators' sparring partners or their sighing fucks, carnal candy for hard men set to do or be done for. Solon became our wise friend, so he had us believe; deceit his liberty. Library of lost books enrolled in his head, he beat Greek poetry into us, my brother Manlius and me, skinny tympana.

In the summer, we conned ancient lines, brambled with obscurities, Pindar's commissioned trademark, on a canvas-shaded slump of rocks where father's fastness pronged the guardian lake. Breezy waves lipped and sipped at the brown shore below what Solonaki termed our "Campanian class-room". One mistake, he clicked Greek reproach with his tongue; the second, down came that switch. He chastised us under licence, master and slave, Manlius more often, and harder, being older. Silence when scourged left my brother our master's master; salved pride. Even when I sprang the right translation, I was tempted to provocative glosses. Solonaki rolled prune-dark eyes upwards, mouthing *po po po,* knowing I knew better, and the switch swished, cruel pleasure. Had we chosen, we could have killed him; no question; and our father us.

Solonaki smiled, one side, when our repetition rang, undeniable as pain, in memory's hairy old ear. *Hod'ex Aitnas...*"; Etna's name salted southern eyes. Solon's family farmed hot terraces above Catania before *ee catastrophe*, when veterans of Marcus Licinius Crassus, Mr Money bagged in general's rig, scavenged rewarding properties, tipped tenants out like night-soil, after the defeat of Spartacus, whom some Sicilians had cheered, others feared. *Men* and *de,* old Greek double act, rhetoric's yoked hauliers – always together, always at odds – divided Hellenes, home and abroad, gave Romans their opening.

Grammar was Solon's solitary legacy. Whoever a man may be, verse plays implacable measurer. Impersonal as the joiner's hinged rule, prosody baffles braggarts, baits bullies, banishes bluff. Alexandria, its lusts and lists, became my grafted fancy, poets' play-ground, lovers' lay-ground. Callimachus, voluminous epigrammatist, recommended brevity: big book, big shit, he said, old friend Apollonius Rhodius in his venomous sights. The Rhodian's Homeric sprawl outlasted C.'s professorial *pinakes* (those hundreds of volumes of scholiastic screed).

Solonaki had us render *Plokamos*, Callimachus' obeisance to Queen Berenice, into Latin elegiacs. Effusive epyllion, it told how she married Ptolemy the Third and as the king went to war in Syria (futile march to wrest the throne for his nephew), Berenice pledged a lock of her hair – "Plok*omos*, accent it right next time, *pethaki mou*"- for his safe return. When the king did indeed reach home once more, the pledged lock had disappeared, later to be divined sparkling a-dangle in the firmament. Solonaki put me on, and away I went:

> "*Observer of every star in the wide sky,*
> *Whose charts clock their rise and set,*
> *The darkening of the sun's bright fire,*
> *The waning of each constellation,*
> *The moon's stolen love-trips from the sky*
> *To Latmos' rocky caves, Conon*
> *Royal astronomer, who cons it all,*
> *Spotted me too, on the sky's threshold,*
> *Lock of Queen Berenice's golden bush…*"

My naughty gloss brought down Solonaki's righteous rod. Having donned Callimachus' pedantic persona like a mask in a comedy, I took Soloanki's switch for cruel congratulation. In truth, untamed Archilochus, five centuries his senior, the bastard bruiser, was my hairy paragon. The pricklier my line, the nearer I was to the long-yarded Parian who pared Homer, held the line; short and sharp, in and out, all prick, hedgehog sergeant the Muses loved and a raucous crow did down, Corax the Naxiot hero whose triumphant cawing riled the gods. The killer pleaded that he had prevailed in fair, if foxy, fight. The Olympian dicasts were amused to despatch him south, to deliver penitential sacrifice at a shrine on Pelops' forefingertip.

Sirmio's narrow throat was clasped by a heavy gate-house, stacked loaves of thick umber stone. Grizzled gate-keepers yielded watchful way to Gaius and Manlius. Swinging deference, away you go then, made the boys toys who, thanks to the parting porters, rode through the archway as if it were not there; brick-bracketed ricochet of hooves proved it was. Then came the dusty beat, bareback, to Verona; "acropolis of Italy" straight-faced visitors dubbed it, implying that they did not rate it all that highly; frontier town, raw not yet weathered walls, hulking new theatre; bastion of demobbed muckers, brazen bully-boys, old sweats done sweating, fourteen-year men who had marched and killed to order, killed for Lucullus, Hellenist and cherry-picker; killed for Sulla, cornelian-faced pricker-out, grandee groper; killed for Pompey, with his permanent wave, wish to please; killed for Julius, pate bald as his prose, gamma for verses, forever on the make and the march, vying to catch Alexander, the greatest.

They stripped us, Manlius and me, with their eyes, virgin booty, those Veronese veterans shooting fuck-you looks. Squaddies' slang – stoopers and stabbers – spiced my gutter lexicon, atlas for navigation up your gonger, dirt road, wet decks. Had it not been for them and their fathers and grandfathers, legions drilled invincible by Gaius Marius's upstart genius, Cimbri would yet be swarming in our fields. Thanks to the New Man's uniformed louts and lechers, the German invaders were compost, thousands upon thousands, in the blood-manured Raudian fields; survivors and fugitive kin corralled beyond the Alps. Taking unearned salutes, one class of smile theirs, another ours, we rode on and out, Manlius and I, branded with vets' hot irony, rough traders with one jeering lesson for the neophyte: get some service in, sonny boy.

Never ask a poet when he first shot a line. They come at any time, troupes of words, bivouac in the mind, conscripts at your service, if you can drill their dance. Father's little boat, *phaselus ille*, shoulder lolling on the chink of shingle, reminded us of where it had been, we not. We pushed it out, Manlius and I, on the lake on fine days, our *parunculus* (happy hapax, apt for piquing pundits); steered – we chose to hold – by Zeus's talkative timber from high oaks on oracular Dodona, en route to fleece the Colchians. Garda's calm seethed in imagination's breeze. The two of us rode out storms under clear skies, salted sweet water, dodged motionless Symplegades, Scylla and Charybdis, embarked the witch Medea, Argo's cargo, herself by Jason bewitched, fratricidal booty, winner's trophy.

We looped homewards, flush with ghosted dreams, past Lesbos, Sappho's byre, self-destroying siren (dumpy girl, they say), threaded the Cyclades, circlet of islands hooping Delos, birthplace of Artemis, mistress of accurate darts, and of brother Apollo, two-edged blade; sacred Delos, no longer errant, lately anchored fast in rock, human merchandise on the hoof racked on that once immortal platter; brains and brawn under the dealer's hammer, podium shaded by the maieutic olive-tree where parturient Leto leaned. Father has shares in the slavers' trade, victors' dividends. We aped servitude and mythic mastery, Manlius and I, then pulled for home, afternoon Argonauts, looking over our shoulders for Sirmio's sharp shingle; pranced ashore, barefoot clever-clogs; June days, jejunior verses:

> "...Flaunted to tempt every heavenly goddess
> When her husband, rich in his marriage,
> Fresh from triumphant wedding night
> (Maiden bride his battle's booty)
> Set forth to conquer Syria."

"Are you looking at me, Master Gaius?"

Back to me, she is stretching cooler-than-marble, black-pitted arms, kallipygous Melissa, white-smiling (I could guess) as she reaches, pinch-assed, tents finger-tipped domestic sheets on wind-biased oleanders, heels up, insteps creased for higher reach, bending ready buds against bobbling bubs, *papillae,* shift with come-and-get-me-knots. Do I tease her, or she me? Did they toss a coin for me, she and Eirene: "Heads or ships?" Which won, which lost? "Come," she says, "*ela, pethi mou, ela mazi mou, me ta megala ommata sou!*" Demotic tongue makes free with me and my big eyes. I fancy her silly and would punish her for it.

"New brides, do they hate love?
Or are the tears they shed outside
The marriage-chamber, that break
Their parents' hearts, all false?
Yes, false compared to the ache
Of Queen Berenice, when her husband
Left for war. That empty marriage-bed, was it,
Grieved you, lady? Or unfeigned dread
Your husband might die that left you
Fainting, superstitious, racked with sobs?
There you were a timid girl again,
And fearing to recall the deed
That proved you strong, a royal stroke
None other dared; murder made you queen!"

She takes his hand, Melissa, mystery's mistress, leads him across courtyard cobbles, fretted with breezy, blood-scabbed feathers, sawdust where outdoor boys twist flapping capon necks, slit screaming pigs. She leads him like a star, Berenice for a day, without looking at him, pretty beast, ripe for blooding. Through the barn door, unshaved planks; hummocks of beady grain silted against the wall, and there she is, slipping her shift, flesh lanced by light from between high tiles, white and black; shadows deeper than flesh.

"Such a girl, to weep such tears as these,
For her husband rub her eyes so raw,
Which gods had power to change you?
That lovers cannot bear to be so long apart?
As your sweet husband went to war, you offered
Me to the powers above, with frightful oaths,
That he come safely home, and back he came,
Asia captive, to Egypt's lands annexed.
And his success made me a star, ancient pledge
Fulfilled in rare new style..."

"*Etimos eeseh? Ready, are you?* Veveos! *Para poly etimos! More than ready! Don't close your eyes, Master Gaius; be a man, be a man; if you can; for as long as you can!*" Whisper of shifting grain under unlatched legs, novice plough, ready furrow. "*You are too! How angry he looks when he gets what he wants. Oh, oh. Oh! Never mind. Start again, can you? You can! What a man, what a...devil!*"

I wished the girl free to want, and be won, not doing a day's work. It made for angry pleasure, the saddled smile, that second, better, longer time. "Take that!" I worked on her, knees upped; "and fill your wet purse," and then the dry rut, tight slipper. "Yes," she said, reached to speed me, clever nails, to spurt; spent men lose, their victory, done. Thank you, damn you, cuntikins.

"Enjoy it, did you?" Manlius said. "Your cherry tart? Why the frown? Sooner I said 'muliebrous muffins'? Of course, you would! Did she...do things you never knew girls did? They all do them."

Gaius put arms around his brother. They held each other – who whose? – then kissed, raced to the slip and into the chuckling lake, knees up, hands up, hands out, lefting and righting the water, pumping quick heels, swam, swam, then burst out, shaking diamond heads in agreement, face to face, identical and unalike. Gaius coughed as they lurched ashore, stretched in the sun, lazy laundry, done: men, never again to be striped by Solonaki; maturity a deprivation.

"Curious, I almost loved her. Wanted her for my own."

"Curiosity helps; almost cardinal; it leaves you free."

"You must be quoting someone."

"Not some tongue-twisting Greek, so you won't know who. Slave in a play. Imagine she's one of father's by-blows, do you, little tight-ass? Or don't you? Both, knowing you."

"I like to imagine...taking her to Etna..."

7

"How long before you pitched her into the crater to immortalise your love?"

"...live in a cottage and write...*Aetna mihi ruptique cavis fornacibus ignes...*"

"Doesn't sound like you, *pethi mou.*"

"Cretans are liars; poets are thieves. Here she comes. She won't look at us, the honey, bet you! Don't look at her."

"She looked at me."

"She did not."

"Proof you did at her."

"Imagine, brother, if it were possible...to be...happy."

"Life in the subjunctive, your idea of happiness, is it, Gaius? Never mine!"

> *"Acme, in Septimius' lap, lover loved,*
> *Holding her close, 'Acme, lost in loving,*
> *You I'll love till the end of time,*
> *Or longer yet! Do I mean it? Do I not!*
> *If I lie, set me head to head, in Africa*
> *Or scorching India, with some tawny lion...'*
> *Is what he said. And Cupid sneezed...*
> *Right and left, there then there, that's the way!*
> *So cued, Acme leans back, light-headed,*
> *Gentles her love's besotted eyes*
> *Kiss-bruised lips, and says,*
> *'Just so, my Septimille mine,*
> *The love I'm slave to, forever, as you to me,*
> *Fierce and fiercer let it flare,*
> *Heat that melts the bones.'*
> *Blessed and happy, off they set,*
> *In amorous unanimity.*
> *Septimius rates Acme, his first, his last.*
> *Better than all your Syrians or Brits,*
> *She promises the joy of joys.*

Who ever saw a two more one?
Could Venus draw a luckier number"

"One apple on the tree, and that unreachable, call that a worthwhile life, *adelphe mou?*"

"A poem's a poem; the poet something else."

"Happiness always means you're missing something."

"And who said that?"

"You will, Gaius, if you ever are, happy."

Sosto, Solonaki used to say, just so. Provincial life fostered serenity, primed impatience; ruddy Rome, the lure, bulged below the horizon. For me, if not for Manlius, privilege doubled with frustration, security with absence from the quick of things. It chafed to be cosseted, supervised with service. Local vanities, provincial scandals had me rehearse insolence that craved metropolitan audition. Penned in cheerful petulance, I versified to tease Archilochus, the wasp, second his sting:

"Wanted by the town of Verona,
Reliable span for a good long bridge,
Braced for dancing. Our old one totters
On dodgy crutches, all set to break its back,
Go splash-bang, flat in the marshes.
Whatever refit you fancy, do it,
Springboard for highland flingers.
But 'prior to building permission'
Greenlight the king of giggles:
One particular Veronese gent
I long to watch plunge, arse over tip,
Where the bog is stinking and boggiest.
They don't come thicker than chummy,
Hasn't the brains of a two-year-old
Snug on dadda's arm. Yet he married
A very young girl, green as a bud

At its greenest, friskier than a kid,
Kid-glove treatment she needed,
Handling saved for the ripest grapes.
Chummy leaves her do as she pleases
Which she's more than pleased to do.
Must have piles, poor poop: never gets
Off his arse! Might as well be alderwood
Scrap, planked in a Ligurian ditch.
He knows as much about what she's up to
As if she'd never existed.
That's my candidate to go flying.
Shock of a good old heave-ho
Might purge stick-in-the-mud's Cat-
atonia. Cf. mule sheds shoe in a swamp."

Gaius Julius Caesar came to Sirmio, tired not sated, after carving another slice of topside Spain; red rivers, local corpses, smoking towns proofs of covetous success, promise of interest due at home. The vanguard's thirsty dust our servants' cue, they smelt it blowing in, knew what they had to do, slicing, slaughtering, for Julius and his mere two thousand or so. Neither tall nor short, roped to ambition's insatiable beat, Julius was one with his men, never a boy, no dandy Gnaeus Pompeius with looks and locks to regulate, middle finger for careful coiffing; Caesar's calvities laurels alone could dress.

Julius claimed Venus as his great-grandmama, randy conqueror, all the ladies' man, yet "Queen of Bithynia", they dared to call him, his triumphant legionaries, cheering and jeering the conqueror who put out, as a stripling, for Bithynia's king and a crust of the oriental loaf. Bawds of a feather, his men, whose fond abuse promised they cared little whom Julie keyed. If it brought him luck, and them, they would do anything for him, tireless adulterer who marched at their head, ho megalos Alexandros ghosting in front of him, the great Alexander who, before his thirsty men, poured his princely pitcher into the desert sand, pulled rank by waiving privilege, as on and on he led them, to the flaming ramparts, Macedon's Achilles, little man, black Bucephalos his high horse, short-lived immortal, history's plinthed divinity, dead before he was divine Julius's present age.

The young Caesar, after Bithynian initiation in provincial service, its ins and outs, was kidnapped when sailing back to Rome. Pirates pulled from their greensleeved Cilician creek, ran down, boarded the lumbering ferry, slung unimportant crew and passengers overboard; sink or swim. How did Julius find cool time to tell his captors that he was worth more alive than all the silly luggage they were rifling? What language (common koine), what promising fingers totted the fat ransom which proved him worth saving? He was their luck, he told them, had the style and smile to convince them to take exceptional care of him. He swore good money would be paid, if they kept him safe; they that it better be, and soon.

A messenger was sent, with Caesar's seal, returned, at length, with evidence that their prisoner did indeed have friends – was crafty Crassus one, already? – willing, with the ready, to bail him out. While they waited, Julius grinned at his captors' brazen stories, posed emulous questions, filed each boasted subterfuge. Did he deign, or disdain, to share and shaft pirated pussy? Be sure he delighted leering brigands with salty stories of the great city, baths they would never see, whose wives he had ridden and which, as quality females preferred, chose to saddle him. How long would Cilician patience last? They teased him, stinking rascals, wound him up with tales of the spit on which they roasted the last hostages whose deceit abused their hospitality.

No sooner than just in time, the Rhodian captain of the pirates' choice steered into their slim anchorage, gold in his locker. They threatened to put the skipper's eyes out, that he might not find his way back, then clapped him on the shoulder, offered wine and calamar *that squatting brown boys had slapped tender on the quay. Ransom counted, Julius on board, anchor up, the pirates called out that they would miss their parting captive. "Don't worry," he replied, "I'll be back. I've marked where to find you and when I do, I'll crucify each last one of you; promise! You know me a man of my word." He was smiling, as they waved get-away hands. A few months later, his flotilla came back and nailed them all. Caesar favoured jokes that he alone could crack.*

Gnaeus Pompeius soon did better, rid the whole eastern Mediterranean of pirates, thanks to the Senate's bounteous commission and its tradesmen sponsors. His clean sweep was achieved quickly enough to win gratitude, never parity, from the boni, *meaning good and rich. Interdicted from the vulgarity of trade, Rome's Old Families were masters of delegated gambles, forever mortgaged investors in distant dabbles. Their surrogates, the merchants and the tax-collectors, could now sail unescorted to and from profitable provinces Gnaeus P. had gone on to confirm as Roman. The second Alexander some called him (Julius not one of them), but no epic advertised his praises, nor prose his cons, not yet. In Judaea, Pompey played judge between contending princelings, last of the Maccabees, and then,* en prince *purloined their prize, divided and ruled Jerusalem, with no more than a hint of force, history's twist, conqueror's screw.*

It took small wit to guess that not a few of the captains who now carried officials in tranquil transit were reconditioned privateers. Pompey offered now-or-never opportunities to enrich themselves, unless they chose to play for higher, dangerous stakes, risk the fate which Caesar had visited on those who entertained him, he them, the last laugher. Gnaeus P. performed for applause from his betters; Gaius Julius, lion in solitary pride, admitted no betters. His own Callisthenes, he would narrate, and rate, Caesar's performance, third-personal egotist.

Not twenty years my senior, Julius, cold, clever eyes, mouth curt as his history, almost forty, Janiceps, looked ahead and over his shoulder, cash and cachet his goals, Venus' martial squire. Pompey, he told us, confidences his gratitude, was lording it in Rome, primus *maybe, but never* inter pares: *in senatorial eyes not quite one of them, Gnaeus had been magnified, in his twenties, and so saluted by the returning L. Cornelius Sulla Felix, general who made his own luck, the East his bank. Did sarcasm spruce the Cornelian salute? Did it not? Stamp my foot, provincial Pompers came to claim, threat and promise, and legions would leap up, ready when he was.*

Flash with success, birth-badged Cornelius flattered the precocious volunteer into domestic dirty work, mop up disloyal Romans (disloyal to Sulla), serve Gaius Marius's officers as they had the Cimbri. Only then was Master P. licensed to go east to Asia, which Sulla's ruthless genius had pacified, and magnify his magnitude, add Bithynia, Pontus and Syria to the tax-collectors' tithing tilth. Julius had gone west to Spain and Gaul; reaped foreign fields for metropolitan revenue, electioneering, circuses, consular promotion.

Was I named for Caesar, father's friend? After what had happened, where and when? Father looked at me, drooped an eyelid at Manlius, let slip, "Your namesake is quite the poet, Julius."

Couched at dinner, Caesar said, "I too am known to try my hand at verses, when I've nothing better to do".

My scowl said nothing *was* better; insurgent cock covert quibble.

Caesar lounges with his provincial friend and his wife, Hisbulla, proper woollen gown, matronly bun, loyal lady, due mother, silent, mundane Hera on her best behaviour. What does the general think of their Cisalpine vintage? Caesar nods as he gulps appreciation; who needs Falernian? Does that semi-smile, one eye scanning her couch, pay Valerius, his host, the compliment of remembered appetite for a younger Hisbulla? Hers for him perhaps? How discreet a proper Roman wife, voteless, voiceless mother of them all!

Watch Manlius, watch Gaius, watching their seniors talking, intimacy their parade; compare and contrast different conclusions brothers draw. Caesar has made friends in southern Gaul, while on the march to and from unyielding Spain. Greek colonists in mercantile Massilia (no libraries there) promise fat unplucked pickings in northern Gaul. Informative deference solicits a percentage of the spoils; new slaves (Greek and Roman hold barbarians common carrion to carry off), estates to fence, towns to found, laws to fix and tax coerced civilians. Caesar means to float on the touts' prospectus, return with commissioned licence to sate or stall creditors, fund popular policies;

racing tortoise, Julius, forever pressing to outflank Macedon's Achilles,
ho megistos Alexandros, *and forever pressed. War needs money, brings*
money, or had better, to the winner and those who back him. Rome's
busiest business is borrowing; its interest conquest, fifteen percent the
going rate, usura *the accelerator.*

Julius tells them how Crassus spent a fortune beating Spartacus and
his gladiator army, fugitives in its train; no glory in crucifying an avenue
of slaves, but promise and threat: Marcus Licinius proving he had
money to spare. When is more than enough enough to sate ambition?
The man who can buy whatever he wants craves triumphs money never
can. M.L.C. paid his philosopher father's moderation the compliment
of greed; like father, unlike son. "Can happen, Valerius!"

Croesus/Crassus has made another superfluous fortune, Caesar tells
them, out of banausic shamelessness, compare Aristophanes' piss-rich
tanner Cleon. Who but Marcus Licinius would think to raise a private
fire brigade, quick with savvy slaves, water-wheelers and dealers? Fires
were commonplace on Rome's wooden hills; Palatine not exempt;
Suburra's tenements regular high-stacked, three-storey tinder. Crassus'
brigade arrived, at the double but not at the fire: next door to it. At first
his leg-man would ask a fee, which fattened as adjacent flames took
hold. Then Marcus had a hotter idea: ask neighbours how much they
wanted for about-to-be-cinders property; then tell them what they were
going to get, pennies. If they agreed, the boys put the fire out; if not,
not. Made of money, Crassus/Croesus grew to own a good deal of
ungrateful Rome. Glory alone had no price, and he would pay it.

"Gaius wants to go to Rome."

"And you must let him, Hisbulla my dear. A Greek can be Greek
anywhere, a Roman only in Rome. You remember the young Marcus
Tullius thought, in new boy innocence, to garner metropolitan kudos
by playing fair with the Sicilians, imagined he would return with
virtuous luggage stamped 'Man to Watch'. When he unpacked, who
was watching? 'Where've you been then, chickpea?' young Publius
Clodius Pulcher asked him, lippy pretty boy's best welcome. 'Visiting

the old folks in Arpinum, is it?' M.T.C. told the story against himself, before others did; and means never to leave Rome again, unless he has no choice. You learn best from people you dread."

Publius Clodius was what Marcus Tullius ached to be, not new but news, the ranking rascal; Claudian cockerel ready to brandish family status to recruit the proles, their votes, their fists, never forgetting what SPQR stood for, S for senate, P for populus, the people, and Q for -que, attached to the people, as it were, if not born to it, apt latch for Caesar, Clodius, Catiline, patrician candidates to head the tail. Who better than a lapsed aristocrat both to play man of the people and to retain the nescio quid, supercilious something, to impress them? Caesar means to shake the heavy Hesperides, make its golden fruits his own; Catiline in mind, he will be Caesar or he will be nothing.

"Going on campaign, are you interested at all, young Gaius? Between verses, it's the only way to rise in the world, carve yourself a rich helping of it."

"He wants only to go to Rome."

"Where he can speak for himself," I said.

"Speak for others first, young man," Julius said. "Or, better, against them. No likelier way in for provincials. Not a man in Rome who matters a fig isn't guilty of something you can't make your name by prosecuting him for. Fleecing a province, bribing voters, buying judges, they all do it; how else does a man get on, and up? Choose your target carefully. Even the smartest poet can make a mess of making a name. Remember what happened to Gnaeus Naevius, that fatal line he shot."

"*Fato Metelli Romae fiant consules.*"

"The boy knows his stuff." Julius looked at me, eyes friendly as green ice. "Implying that the Metelli get made consuls because destiny makes them so, never their merits. Dangerous clan, branches everywhere, still prone to take consulships as their due. Naevius mocked their presumption, presumed cleverness could get away with it. Exit Naevius. Not so clever. Prosaic Marcus Tullius aimed more shrewdly. True, Verres was connected to the Metelli, but his greed was too loutish not to embarrass the quality. What fun friend Tully had, claiming that, when governor, Master V. emptied Sicily of its treasures!"

"Guides showed people where the statues had been, and none now were."

Julius smiled. "Clever boy knows it all; which always leaves a man with a thing or two to learn."

Solonaki had told us the story, failed to smile at it.

"I dined with Verres in Massilia," Caesar is saying, "more than once; shipped his ripest pickings up there in good time, thanks to a reliable Rhodian skipper and his commodious bottom. Good table he keeps, Gaius V.; best oysters I ever tasted this side of Sergius Orata's Lucrine lake. Master V. had already removed the pearls, no doubt. I tipped him with gossip, who tops and tups whom in the restless bed of the Palatine. An exile may take his stash with him, sit pretty and still crave the jiggle-cum-giggle of metropolitan small talk. Friend Verres shrugged, not surprised, when he heard Marcus T. was the going (and coming) favourite for the consulship. He hopes Catiline will pip him, but fosters no loud grudge, accepts Chickpea seized the chance to loud-pedal his rhetorical wares (trimmed by another Rhodian master, land-locked this time, professor Posidonius). Gaius Verres ain't ashamed of notoriety. Fame's caricature requires small upkeep. He sits pretty, unblistered feet cushioned on a satchel of loot, and waves me lucky as I march back and forth in front of him. His money's on Catiline, for fun. Exiles root for long shots, quick returns. Ever meet Lucius Sergius, did you? Great sport, prince of stirrers; Rome loves a reckless rascal until it don't. Broker than I am, Lucius, and nothing like as...circumspect. He plumped for Sulla, as I for Gaius Marius, but never got fat on it. Now he's loud for the common people and cancelling their debts, and incidentally his own."

"Can't-stop gambler, I gather."

"Remind me, my dear Valerius, why else a man sets sail for distant Colchis."

"Grant you that one," my father said, "been there a couple of times myself," briefly a man I scarcely recognised, scavenger's humour in his eye, predating paternity.

"And here's the pretty pelt!" Julius waved his hand at our Greek-statued hall, his gesture including, as if by chance, a fair-haired slave girl Phoenissa, finger-bowl in hand, with the brazen bloom to look back at him. "Your chaps are looking after my men very well, Valerius," Julius said, "judging from the rumpus. When you get to Rome, young Gaius, have a care whom you lampoon to get yourself talked about. The Metelli are still makers and breakers. Our friend Caecilius Celer is all set to add to their roster of consuls. Able chap, too much celerity – quickly in, quicker out – to please his wife. Quite a hostess, the beautiful Clodia, haven't enjoyed her spread myself, too busy. She loves theatricals. Why the lean smile, young Gaius? Kindled appetite's wick, have I, possibly?"

My mother wrapped her long silence around her and, with a lift of the hand, parting salute, implying enough, but no offence, left the room, Phoenissa with her, trailing a look.

Caesar said, "Young Caelius Rufus will mark your boy's card, Valerius. Expensive, Rome, these days. Between votes and vetoes, a man needs a fortune if he wants to get on in politics."

"He doesn't," I said. "He prefers books."

"You said. And the sex; am I wrong?"

"Great Caesar wrong?"

"We don't run to fortunes," my father said.

"I do rate that Sabine accent of yours, Valerius, when money's mentioned."

"Introductions he could do with."

"Ways in are easy. Ways out you'll have to fashion for yourself, young man. The ladies rarely take exits well unless their own instep impels them. Where do you plan to live?"

I said, "Anywhere."

"Never the right address. I let it be bruited that I have a place in the Suburra, among the dribs and the drabs, for the votes it gets me, the common touch. Not there very often. A man can stand only so much of the salt of the earth with the wind behind it. Lodge in my nest, young Gaius, if you will, cry cuckoo till you land a better. I'll scratch you a word for Publius Clodius; straight as an eel, knows everybody back to front, and *vice versa*, quite a speciality of his, coming and going, they tell me, then doing it again. In Rome, a man is told everything; unwise to credit anything but the unsavoury. Only our dear friend Marcus Tullius thinks that things would be as they should be if they could only be as they used to be, which they never truly were. The Palatine's where to trawl and troll, young Gaius, if papa's tin trickles that far uphill, somewhere you can breathe the airs the best people give themselves. Good for that cough of yours."

His charity made me cough again. I lacked stamina to march with his legions and he guessed as much; his kindness stuck in my throat. As grateful for favours as I resented condescension, I hoped he would stay a while, if only that I might advertise my indifference. I made no effort to see him the next morning, but I was in good time to do so. Sometimes one walks with oneself as with a stranger.

> *"I'm not all that interested, Caesar J., whether I please you*
> *Or not. Who are you, pray? Mister Black or Mister White?"*

A writer has no call to dislike anyone in order to declare his independence by a show of get-me, fuck-you lampoonery. What neat phrase in Latin's lock-stepped language lacks serrated edge? Accuracy and exaggeration work adjacent shifts. Slave and free fed from, contribute to, common idioms. Seemliness cloaked grievances, courtesy power. What Roman grew up in a household with slaves and was not soon alert to duplicities threading politeness and menace, formality and behind-the-scenery, complacency and vigilance in every domestic tapestry? Banter hinted at Saturnalian laxity; patrician diction tightened stitches, threatened stripes.

"Young Gaius."
  "Sir?"

"Rome. I can see you're handsome enough, and clever enough I don't doubt, but...are you hard enough, do you suppose?"

"To do what, sir, exactly?"

"To do whom, sir, to be exact. You don't like me, do you?"

"Sir, I respect you greatly –"

"And nimble enough to temporise. Good for you, *pro tem.* Scorn and ambition; dress the one as the other and you just might make your mark in the shitty of shitties, as the shmarter shenatorials shay. Publius Clodius is worth knowing just for his imitations, man of the peep-hole, he calls himself, eyes it all. Despise them as you will; cultivate them you must, the quality I mean. One can't help loving it, if never quite as much as it loves itself. Take Marcus Porcius for example; and don't strain to bring him back. I've made you smile. Forgive me. More than he ever does."

I had smiled to hear the great man produce a slice of matutinal ham; can it be that I made him nervous? Envious: the hair.

"Mount your betters' ladies, young Gaius, when you scale the Palatine, but mind your back when you're doing it. Entrances and exits, careful which is which. Ups can also be downs."

"Heracleitus made the point," I said.

"And you had to tell me so, clever boy. Not so clever can be cleverer still. You mean to be a man of hot and honest passions. Straight as a die, don't they say? And the straight often die of it. One last word of good advice for you to ignore: when in Rome, trust no one you don't owe money to. Creditors are the only people with a practical interest in keeping a man alive. Pay them off and you risk they'll put paid to you. You're minded, I suspect, to scarify your betters. We all have similar wishes, or had; but allow me to tell you what you may not care to hear. In Rome, words can made you famous, sometimes feared, but only money and power bring respect among Latins. Seek temporal office as well as immortality and you'll make a more lasting mark. My centurions have an old squaddy's line when it comes to barrack-room lawyers who rail against the system. The system's the system; but that's not the line I mean. 'Farting against thunder' is the one I had in mind."

"Heracleitus of Ephesus made bold to say
You can never step in the same river twice;
The same shit, he'd better have added,
You always can."

I was glad to see Caesar gone; but he left his mark on me. I thought less of my father, whose unsmiling jaw had always made him look so granitic. The man whose fortune had been built on giving nothing away was belittled by showing himself so proud to have his hospitality taken for granted. It hollowed a furtive scheme in me, Promethean duplicity: steal his fire in a fennel funnel, rig impudence with filial respect. Genuine becomes calculated with but an iota of subscript difference: I smiled more often at my mother.

Caesar honoured republican protocol, furloughed his army north of the Rubicon and reached Rome, solus ipse, in time to witness Cicero's braggadocio after he had pipped Lucius Sergius Catilina for the consulship. The bad loser went for broke, gimcrack Gracchus, two brothers rehearsed as one (Lucius killed his junior, they say, in a temper, pettish Romulus). Chancer with a crumby purse, none of the substance of Athenian Solon, Sergius staked everything he didn't have on another seisachtheia, *promised to tear up the people's We-Owe-Thems, make himself the cleanest sweeper of the city's slates, his own not least.*

Marcus Tullius, when young and hardly known, played defiant defender of the Sicilians despoiled by Gaius Verres, risked Naevius' fate by taking on the Quality that his own eloquence auditioned to join. The same (but different) M.T.C., now cast as consul, when it came to indicting Sergius Catiline, played to a patrician gallery of whom, thanks to their nods, he was licensed, in his own esteem, to count himself one. Cicero took his own advancement and their applause, when he proposed what they wanted to hear, as proof of the senators' moral discrimination. Rhodian rhetoric spiced his war/rant. Senators smiled and smirked: how hard he worked to be one of them and so proved that he was not! Cato's praise, all but unalloyed, thus not, would have been a sweet certificate of accession. Cicero had his small revenge: he spotted the righteous Cato reeling home drunk and whispered it, loudly, as proof that Marcus Porcius was also human. "You never know what the late evening has in store," Tully quoted, and had to add, "or the early morning, come to that!"

Too wary to be of Catiline's risky party, follow-my-leader never his game, Caesar still appreciated Sergius, the dandy dash, folly's flourish; did his legitimate best to save his and his friends' hides, but went no further. Cicero put his armour on, once putsch came to shove and he had learned that Catiline and most of his crew, some armed, many not, had quit the city. Caesar – wide chunk of swarthy Spain in his pouch – prated like a profitable patriot, rehearsed the law that forbade Roman citizens being put to death, by the gross, without trial. What else had his mentor Gaius Marius done, and his enemy Cornelius Sulla, when citizens could be pricked and pillaged? Caesar's booty-fattened soldiers, en civile, paraded loyal muscle in the street, advertised services he had rendered the republic, their own availability for unfinished business. Knowing they would see him right, he could afford a show of ominous rectitude.

Cicero favoured the Good, as old school senators termed themselves, having a lien on the goods that Catiline craved. Cicero, who flattered or fulminated, anything to win his case, the lawyer's law, took his betters' speciousness for specie. The advocate nobbled nobles, flattered fame, won cases, not campaigns; took rewards, won no spoils, gained no lieges or legionaries. Buoyant bombast could impress, sometimes amuse, but what fourteen year-men ever stood by M.T.C. usque ad...as far as he dared or cared to lead them? Electing Tully "parens patriae", father of his country, the senators framed the hero of the hour, and made nunky theirs, if never one of them: did "parens" not carry a hint of obedience to their lordships, pareo, parere..? Caesar meant, in time, to have no masters, take no baited hook. He would be forever in uncancelled, unacknowledged debt to Sergius Catiline, scapegrace Remus, jumping jack, whose adventure taught Julius what he must never do: fail.

Did Marcus Porcius Cato guess that when Caesar called on his peers to honour the letter of the law, knowing they would not, he was as good as warning them that, when he came to top the ladder, all those impatient rungs, he would never leave it to them to be his judges? Marcus Porcius moved to execute Catiline and his friends less to support Cicero than to finger Caesar, the nascent menace (and – did he guess? – Cato's someday nemesis).

Cicero prevailed, mercilessness seconded by Crassus and company, pro bono publico, for the good of the people, more importantly, the good people, those who counted, never on their fingers. Caesar was careful, with seemingly incautious scruples, to remain within the circle of rectitude quite as if Popilius Laenas – who hooped Antiochus IV Epiphanes, divine pretender, in a dusty circle, dared him not to be a friend of the Roman people, and then came home to do for the Gracchi – were still alive to infringements of prescribed propriety. Laenas past and Laenas future, simple woollen name cloaked two sharp men, one who had been, one to come, Mark Antony's bandwagoner, who did for Marcus Tullius and nailed his eloquence, severed tongue and hands. Later comes sooner than you think.

Caesar defended Catiline by upholding republican precedent: citizens should never be condemned to death without due and individual process. Cicero was armed with the last-word, catch-all warrant, senatus consultus ultimum: do what needs to be done to save the republic (as we, The Good, define it). Even during the debate in the Curia, consular lictors stood sentinel at the New Man's side; steel ready to be unsheathed, at a nod, to put full stop to equivocation. Caesar's speech was delivered with no stentorian bray, hands as discreet as Pericles'; an aide-mémoire was being posted, unblinking eyes on Cicero who had but to give the word and consign the quondam Marian to history's unvisited necropolis. Caesar rallied no loud senatorial faction, but did Cicero see an augury in Venus, unforgiving goddess, perched in Julius's family tree?

Marcus T. wore only the annual braid of office. Caesar, unthreatening and precise, quick on his feet, bold and conservative, aptly laconic, answerable only with gravity, such a man made the

consul his admirer even as he, Julius, threatened to be Tully's sometime benefactor. "Cedant arma togae" *was Marcus T.'s officious prayer, but when did arms ever yield to toga before toga capitulated and became a victor's civil camouflage?*

Cato watched, prig in the middle, censorious great-grandfather at his shoulder. His daughter, Porcia, would marry Marcus Brutus; Sulla's Fausta Titus Annius Milo; Fulvia, widow of Publius Clodius, Marcus Antonius; and would live to gloat, later still, over Tully's mutilated corpse. Women wove secret strands, laced and lanced the Roman world.

Publius Clodius Pulcher, dragueur *and drag-artist, liked Lucius Sergius Catilina, the nerve, the verve; Pretty Boy too spoke out against group anathema, but did not long lament the chancer-in-chief when he died,* le beau Serge, *brave few thousand with him, not enough weapons to go round, all wounds in front, spendthrift Spartans at their unsung Etrurian Thermopylae. All said, all not yet done, Marcus Porcius proposed that Cicero be known as unique father of his country. Who but an upstart is flattered by being put in a class of his own? But, yes, Marcus Tullius was the man of the hour ("Not without cause," said Brutus, "but not without end"): it was to have fewer minutes than Chickers presumed when he said of the conspirators "Vixere", his one monosyllabic speech, meaning "they have lived", i.e. were dead.*

Cicero took pride in being named an augur, antique honour bestowed on those who, supposedly, divined the future from sacrificial offal. He owned that one of the once sacred fellowship could not pass another in the street without a covert smirk that confessed scepticism about the activity which distinguished them. Happily unable to divine his own fate, Tully took pride in co-option not least because it made him the collegiate peer of Quintus Hortensius Hortalus, brightest star of the Roman bar before the man from Arpinum came to town and won his triumphant case against Verres, whom Hortensius defended. The two advocates became learned friends, mutual flatterers who never quite trusted each other; why else the flattery? Hortensius followed Lucullus, another retired idol, becoming both gardener and gourmet.

He watered his plane trees with wine, to fatten their foliage, announced his social ascendancy by being the first man in Rome to serve peacock at an augural feast. Thanks to the growing appetite for gastronomic evenings, where scurrilous dwarfs added salt in gossip form, the price of a good chef came to exceed that of a horse.

However many moons later, Gaius Valerius Catullus makes ready to take the Via Flaminia south. By way of an envoi, he comes across Eirene, down on neat knees, swabbing a mosaic floor and takes her without a word, endorsing mastery. She never lets go of her rag, offers "Oh! Oh!", and goes on polishing the doorstep roundel of Venus and Adonis, black and white, head down, smile only for herself, Sphinxy minx. He would have her look back and up; free not to, she does not: a liberty. Her breasts seem larger.

"What do you bet she didn't know whether it was you or me?"

"You flatter yourself! All in a day's work, poor bitch. They come; we go."

"I shall miss you, Manlius. I wish you were coming with me."

"Make your mark, Gaius, then I will, and you'll be pleased to see me, almost. Travel safely, dear bro."

"And you, *adelphe mou*, come back with your shield, not on it. Or, like Archilochus, without it."

"What's to be sad about? Knowing you, you'll find something."

"I'll bet she did; know who."

Months later, Eirene bled to death in the barn, scabbed the stiff straw. They saved the pupa, *bawling girl; small change, whoever the father.*

Crossing the Rubicon, jaundiced divide, decisive dribble, I was on my way past more dried, perhaps still drying, blood and wormy guts than I chose to think about, minded only to make my mark in Rome, armed with a satchel of words. Die cast, solitary buccaneer, I entered the city, smelt its appetites and their cloacal consequences, quartered its quarters, savoury and otherwise; poets and low life have old affinities. The best people paraded dead ringers to live up to; staring ancestral images lined their halls, whose estates their pockets. Fortunately, the *gratin* like to have their wits about them, poets and playthings, to dress their tables, sing public praises, peddle private potions and poisons. I had never threaded a free woman.

I dossed in Caesar's house, lorded it as if he owed me something. Cornelius Nepos had a library I was free to scrutinise (Aeschylus's comedies my favourites, the clever allusiveness, playful indeed). I haunted poetry readings. Where else to mock and mimic the going vatic warble, discover which scribblers' backs to scratch, whose flaunted tails to twist? Fabullus, vicar of Fabulinus, divine chat*meister*, prescribed a dose of Calvus: Master C. talked as well in the courts, he told me, as he sang for his suppers, if I cared to discover how high the highest hurdles. Higher than he was, I discovered: had Gaius Licinius been a line of verse, he would have stretched barely to a pentameter. After his reading, sweetly pitched, I grant, he came up to me, all five feet of him, ambition taller.

"I hope you enjoyed yourself."

"When there was you to enjoy Gaius Licinius? I did tick the margin of your number about Alexandrians dividing the rounded moon 'like brothers,/ Each sure his half is bigger than the other's'. I do rate a shententious rhymer."

What quicker way to a poet's heart than quoting him back to himself? Calvus's lifted lip, wrinkled nose, promised that I was passing, almost, for metropolitan. "Implying that you could do better?"

"If I ever do half as well, I shan't have to jump into Etna, shall I?"

I relished the contraction of his brow, before he said, "Empedocles was that? Your allusions flatter me; very wise! Country boys should always bring their trowels with them and lay it on thick." He had his chin up, nose in air, the pug. "Thirsty? I am. *Salax taberna* time; nothing like the low life, unless you have no choice but to live it. Let's cut!"

Lofty little man, chin stuck out to make him taller, his strut licensed me to defer when he waved away my skinny purse and paid the Transtiberine tavern-keeper who produced a dish of fish, freshly caught, he promised, from "between the two bridges". My provincial frown gave me away. "In other words," Calvus said, "just above Tiber island and just below where the public sewer flows into the river. Flavours you won't find anywhere else. *Buon app!*"

"I did rate that number you quoted about archer Paris in the sack with Helen. He gives her the full quiver and…she yawns! Archilochus, did you say? Never heard it before."

"Not surprising," he said. "I ran it up last night. Home-made antiquity. Speciality of mine, stealing what ain't there. Nothing shines like pristine counterfeit. All literature is second cousin to a swindle."

The tight bar – marble slab pierced with craters, for all but as good as Samian wine and Cerignola olives – was holed like the public jakes on the Janiculum where you might squat alongside a flush of *boni,* more honest dirt issuing from broad bowels than ever from mean mouths. Wit enough to solicit emulous ingratitude, Gaius Licinius took generous pride in introducing me to everybody I needed to know, flashed my trail to better things, to mark his own *superbe.*

> *I had to laugh. A grockle in the gallery,*
> *Catching our Calvus in full flow*
> *Holds up his hand, amazed, and has to say,*
> *"Heavens, can't the little bugger talk?"*

"*Salaputium* am I?" he said, next time we met. "Where did that one come from?"

"Bottom of the barrel, where else? Never met a saltier little operator than you, my dear."

He put his arm through mine. "I was going to ask you to Clodia Metelli's thrash next week."

"And was I going to come?"

"Onward and downward, that your sorry scheme? Bloody well come, bloody well like it. Before the play. Publilius's new number. Reheated Menander with the names changed, if I know that little Syrian smoothy. Epigrams relined while you wait. Small drinks party."

"Just a few people is that?"

"Lots of people," Calvus said, "small drinks."

"I gave you that one. Am I expected?"

"Unexpected, which is very much madam's kind thing. No promises, mind. In Rome promises are like a *taverna*'s cheap crockery: there to be broken."

"You're riding me, I can feel jockey heels nudging my kidneys."

"Hold yourself fortunate to be mounted, my dear." We had to stand aside on the sidewalk as a flock of sheep were urged on their way by a lame countryman. "On their way to vote Caecilius Metelli consul," Calvus said. "Clodia's *marito*."

"Who else is as flash with an anapaest, as you are, Gaius C., that I ought to con? Anyone?"

"Any number, so they like to think. Come back with me and I'll wrap you a florilegium of old fish and you can say hullo to my Quintilia. See how lucky I am; save your appetite for other apertures. That I mean."

"See under true love, its witless edge."

"Careful, country boy! Narcissus can always drown in a puddle of his own pissing. Remember that, Gaius Valerius."

Quintilia was a pretty woman, in the happy early months of pregnancy. In the letter I wrote to Manlius that same evening, I told him, "You could see right away what the little man likes about his lady: he grows a full six inches the moment he sees her."

> *"Unless I loved you, Calvus, more than my eyes,*
> *Simpaticissimo signor, I'd skin you for this*
> *Anthology of Latin weeds, like your*
> *Vatinius. What have I done – or said –*
> *That merits stuffing with verse like these?*
> *May the gods rain havoc on whoever*
> *Lumbered your good self with this*

Emetic repertoire. Guest editor?
Cornball Sulla is my guess, the litera-tourist.
I'll do you a favour, gladly, just to prove
You didn't take all this trouble for nothing.
Ye Gods though, what tumtitty-tum
To serve addressed to 'Dearest Catullus mine'!
Just the job, you say? To put me to sleep that is
On this day of days, the Saturnalia!
Don't rub it in. Just wait for the comeback:
Soon as it's light in the morning, I'm off
To remainder-land: Caesius, Aquinus,
Suffenus – every toxic scribbler I can find
To rack you with; for the all-thumbs crew,
The thumbscrew they so loudly merit.
Meantime, club-footed poets, out you go!"

I read my tripping tropes to a clutch of Calvus's set, none of them slated in my "worst/iary" as Lucius Varus called it. "Rely on ambition for pitiless pitch," he told me, "the kind that sticks; but beware the slings and arrows of the unamused. No one cares more about what's said about him than the man who claims not to have heard it. A poet can be too quotable for his own good. Ask anyone you like; easier to find than anyone who likes you. People rarely forgive what they fail to forget."

I thanked Julius's friend, just, for his monitorial quip, ignored it, and fired the following to Lucius by return:

"Your chum Suffenus is at it again, Lucius V.,
Agreed he's nobody fool, has charm, talks well,
Writes the longest, longest verses in the world,
Ten thousand lines, I reckon, if not more,
Crown octavo, virgin papyrus, flash binding,
Hand-ruled, pumiced perfection; and now...
Read on. Man about town, smartyboots
Suffenus turns goat-sucker, sewer-rat.

Hold your nose and tell me how smart-ass,
Or whatever is smarter than that,
Turns rustier than a rustic, the clod,
The moment he fingers a dactyl.
Yet enraptured when a pome he pens,
Happy as happy, Narcissus the bard!
No big surprise: who's not a Suffenus
Somewhere along the line? Who isn't blind
To what's incapsulated on his spine?"

The forum and its *viavai* make Rome a metropolitan village. No grandee escapes scrutiny, he hopes; no bladder its prick. I watched Marcus Tullius coming down the high street, *Via Sacra*, pat patter on paternal lips, pristine morning edition of his famous self, stretched neck, longing to see round some people the better to pick out those who might matter. He advanced in brisk *rallentando*. In a hurry to stay in sight as long as custom and compliments were available, eminence and – hullo! – wariness marched in tandem. Why? The approaching answer: Publius Clodius, prancing, all but dancing, past the speakers' rostrum, loud black hair, making recognition alone a form of compliment.

Caelius Rufus the red-head, closer, caught my eye. His look and looks promised intimacy to any he chose to light on. "The very man," he said; and *"nemo verior, vereor"* (none verier, I fear), I had to cap him. Caelius drooped an eyelid, apt to kindle an instant impression that he and his target, male or female, had a common past, if only in the future. Amused attention quick to assess weakness, tickle selected trout, when you expected Red to blink, or look elsewhere, he was still there, full face, delivering a seemingly exclusive self; confidences worth your favour, depend on it, if you lack the wit to trump them.

"There you have him, Chickpea *dans ses oeuvres*," Publius C. proclaimed, to no one in particular. Long-wristed, double-jointed gestures bid everyone welcome to his camp. "New man, old man, complete with cronies and clients, postulant posse to prove that he's the greatest man in Rome, proof the greatest scorn to solicit. Our leading civilian, voted patter *patriae,* Rome's biggest mouth, never braver than the day he wore his breastplate, charged into battle, in the Curia already, flashed martial mettle to the senators, tongue the swellest muscle in his armoury. Clean old hands clapped the climber who'd do their dirty work, one of them what wasn't; if only *noblesse* obliged, he'd be among them, he dared to presume. Forever persuading himself that the good old days are just around the corner. I shall have him presently, my masters; the way he looks at me, not looking, promises he knows I shall. Why? Why not?"

Cicero's reaction? Not to react. Clodius had him forked, if not yet toasted. He looked or he did not look; either was as good, or bad, as a fall. Caelius, at my elbow, seconded and contradicted Clo-clo's nasty tease, quite as if we were close friends already: "Dear old Marcus T., he do so love the grand manner, the laughs it raises, the tears it brings to his own eyes, applause he can deprecate and augment. Mr Verbosity, the quality call him, behind his back. Promise to write him a letter, he'll have written you two before you start."

"You don't entirely like him?"

"Mr Verbosity? I love him, Gaius Valerius, like a father…"

"And no further?"

"Notch yourself for that one. He's taught me everything I know about courtroom tactics, has *misterissimus*; never allows a superlative to go out on its own. Stretches a point like a Parthian's bow. Poke your learned friend in the eye with your stylus and assume he'll wink at you for it, that's Tully. The shrewdest, best-informed intelligence in Rome. Listen to his advice with the greatest respect; then do the opposite."

The words shaped for me carried to Publius, and were meant to. "Yes," he said, "always walks forward squinting sideways, master Chickers, do you notice, Caelius? Of course you do, you bitch! Out-of-town townee, playing Capitoline goose and gobbling for the job." Clodius was doing his Cicero for me, confecting instant intimacy, cheeking Caelius. "Am I interrupting? I hope so. No welcome like a scowl! That turns into a smile, thank you, darling, whoever you are."

"Gaius Valerius Catullus."

"I know that, Caelius, don't I, dear Gaius? He wants to have got to you first, hot for virgins, unbeaten tracks, ruby conman, that's Red! Julie C. told me to look out for a handsome ephebe with a hayrick of hair, Cisalpine straw between his teeth. Sticking his neck out, look at him, Marcus T., attention's all he asks! His betters his debtors now, he likes to suppose. And are they? Go tell the Spartans; will they care to know? Civilian victories smack of sharp legal practice, isn't it?" That "isn't it?", with attendant twitch of the nostrils, beckoned me into Clodian argot; *dhen einai etsi?* Ah, dem Gricks! I flinched and was flattered. He put a hand on me, a Delian auctioneer's next item I might have been. I liked it and also I did not. "Who but an outsider," he said, "tries so... *effusively* to parade the nobility the noble have long had up for sale? All homage smacks of parody, who said that?"

"Calvus, it has to be."

"Half-pint totes a gallon of words, give him that. Keep it nice and nasty, Gaius V., the future'll open like a lady's private purse, always a softer touch than you think. Careful what you sheathe with the sex though: what you put in comes out lighter. Onwards and upwards is Tully's motto, but where can he go from up, but down? First the plum, then the plummet. The future, my dears, belongs to the grockles, and their flatterers. Way down way up. Heracleitus, sour aristo, had it right. Why else do I plan to be adopted as a pleb, if I can swing it? Swinging is my best turn, isn't it? Qualify as tribune of the oiks, I shall be up on that rostrum giving today's top dog tomorrow's boot, am I right? And be damned to their sullen constitution! Everything comes to those who don't wait, were you going to say? No? It must have been me."

I said, "Who's the *misterissimus* whom Marcus T. seems almost... grateful to patronise?"

"Shorten and sharpen, Gaius V., and you'll be amongst us in a trice or a triolet. Avoid 'seems to'; strike before they see you draw. Unseemliness beats '*esse videatur*' to the punch. Steal their lightning, their thunder they can keep, isn't it? Said swagger gent is my semi-bro-in-law, none other than, with names to parade: Quintus Caecilius Metellus Celer, never clever, but don't bother to say so. My sister Clodia's lauded lord. As in *the* Clodia, which is not where he can often be found, if all be known, and it usually is, most of it, before it's halfway round the block. Going too farced for you, am I? And go I must, to cozen a consular or two. I leave it to Red to mark your card. Depend upon it, handsome, you couldn't be in worse hands, that's how lucky you are, isn't it? Be good until you can do better. Come and throng my door of a morning. You can learn a lot from the toadies' croak, get street, my dear; make a name they can sing."

"Just the place, they tell me, your halls, to complete my pedication."

"Do they so? Their names please, on a plate, and I will serve them right. Top and bottom. *Ave atque vale,* take your pick and stick it." He clasped my genitals, weighed them, not bad, smiled and went, new old friend: "To be continued," floated over his shoulder. And then: "All insolence smacks of homage."

"And all arrogance of crawling," I threw back to him over the attendant heads.

While Publius gave me the honour of a get-away wave, Caelius was bowing, one-sidedly, to the descending Marcus Tullius. "My dear fellow," said the great one, well-versed when it came to pulling newcomers to his side, introducing him at the same time: "Caelius Rufus, excellent young man, father an *eques honestissimus atque divitissimus.*"

"No call to unsheathe your shiniest cutlery, my dear Tully, I know the gentleman," Celer said. "How are you Rufus? Father well, I hope. My salutes to him. Come and see me." The senator linked arms with Cicero; on they went, smug as Scipios.

"Check the flea in my ear," Caelius said. "Better see Celery's wife, before she sees you, our metropolitan wolverine. Marcus Tullius did master C. a favour, so he thought, putting him in at the sharp end when it came to nailing Catiline and co. He does favours to his betters, the better to be owed them."

"Mark of the climber, giving a leg-up to people above him, isn't it?"

"Marcus Chic's not so secret wish was always to be the toff that Sergius C. was born, and be rated such, not least by said smarty, as he certainly was, up to a point. I was half in love with him myself, cocky Catters, the top half."

"Half in love, what kind of love is that?"

"The best; in and out, ask Clodia Metelli, nicely; Rome's queen bee; makes a season's honey of the best, then buzzes off."

"Threat or promise, is that?"

"If riddle are no incentive, what are Sphinxes for?"

"Rome seems a lot calmer than I was threatened, and promised."

"Much duller now Lucius Sergius is rotting in his Etruscan ditch. Poor Tully, precociousness does age a man! He wanted Sergius to have been a bad, bad neoteroid. In truth, he was no worse than ill-starred and out of chips; not as many friends as his handsome mirror promised. Never trust your own smile."

"Not everyone who couldn't say no to him was promising yes, was that it?"

"Many cheered, fewer marched. That was indeed very largely it, Gaius V.; baldy among them; me too. Odds not good enough. Always beware a betting man."

"Is it wise to say as much?"

"Julius has the wit to take today's sarcasm for tomorrow's compliment. Sound plan to broadcast what men might otherwise whisper. They'll then find something else to be the first to tell people. Tully taught me that, not that he meant to. He hates Publius because Clo-clo's *sotto voce* threatens to carry further than his *f-f-fortissimo*, Tully's, isn't it? Publius makes light, heavily, of that famous 'Middle Way'; no traffic on it except Marcus T., marshalling what ain't there be to marshalled. Moderation's sword is blunt on both edges. *Cher maître* C., watch him clap Gnaeus Pompey on the shoulder, don't you love it? One *arriviste* makes another at home, where neither quite is. The Concord of Men of Good Will, and bad wont as Publius flash-boy has it; high-class low life Tully can never be is Clo-clo, aristo gutter-boy who won't never take nunky for a gent, just as his sister wouldn't, as a lover; she's quickly bored, but tires of slowly; are you with me, Veronese?"

"Be careful, Caelius, with your epithets."

"And not be Caelius, Transpadane *signore*?"

"Last time you call me that with that heavenly set of teeth."

"No, no, master G.! I do the whacking here. I'm playing tutor, ain't I? Julius said I should. Sooner I did it in Greek?"

"*Malista,*" I said. "Do you always do as Caesar asks?"

"Unless and until crass Crassus tilts his cornucopia in my lap."

We were watching Cicero's concluding salutation to Metellus Celer, who made it seem a favour to consent to be favoured.

I said, "I always thought Chickpea a byword for conjugal propriety."

"When did always last forever? Familiarity is pleasure's dust. Terentia was the *arriviste*'s idea of a prize, who prized him less for periodic rehearsing in her bed. He rates his slave boy, Tiro, higher, who has no choice but take dictation till the closing clausulae. Daughter Tullia is Chicker's truest treasure. He thinks she's too good for anyone without a hall full of vacant staring seniors. He'll likely end up marrying her to some bone-head with a fruity family tree and a worm for a wick."

"Clodia's sisters...."

"Not a bad plan! Make a play for one, or the other, or both, and watch for madam with the eye in the back of your head."

"Are they as...sociable as she is?"

"One is nice; the other nicer. They are as they are in the light of what she is, never the other way round. When you look at Clodia, she sees herself; that's who she keeps her secretest smile for. Play her like a fish, if that's your pleasure; never suppose she isn't playing you. Enjoy what she gives you access to, while she does; put your heart on your hook and you'll never get it back."

"No lure like a warning."

"Better serve her purposes than have any of your own, other than amusement. Practise your charms; whatever's offered, it'll be for her pleasure, never yours."

"Had your season with her, do I gather?"

"Pleasures ahead," Caelius said. "Meanwhile, come and be civil to my current charmer. Ipsitilla, the very girl. Put her name in your agenda. No skin off my doodle. She rates double-parking, if you've got the gall, Cisalpine lover-boy. I go one way and you the Persian. We can toss."

"My subject? The future tense of love,
Delectable Ipsitilla, clever darling,
Have me report to you this very afternoon.
Your answer's 'copy that'? Then pray be sure
No one gets to your door and shoots the bolt before me.
Forget that itch to go shopping;
Stay right, and tight, where you are; devise
A menu; nine helpings on the trot.
I have the appetite; do you? Then flash the word:
I'm bored stiff alone, Flagstaff Hill in the bed."

And then again, a day later, still rooty, after a solitary night:

"A humble request, if you're not too busy:
What shady spot are you hiding?
We've got search-parties out in the park;
Ditto the circus and the bookstalls,
And hallowed ground (Jove's on the Capitol).
I did a private walk-about myself,
Polled the ladies round Pompey's Porch.
All unblinking innocence, my dear.
'Come on,' I insisted, 'Camerius,
You wicked, wicked girls, what's up?'
One of them made a clean breast of it:
'Here he is,' said she, down with her dress,
'Between my pretty titties, skulking, see?'
Hercules would labour keeping up
With you. You've gone too bloody far.
Give us a hint where we can find you.
Out with it, coraggio, rise and shine!
What posse of creamy darlings have you
Under arrest? No comment, do you say?
Keep shtumm, you junk the pick
Of the crop. Venus blesses a man

Who can both kiss and tell.
No dice? Stay buttoned if you must,
Just give me a taste of who you're up to!"

The day came. I heard her before I saw her, her laugh, the chuckle, *dulce ridentem.* It steepened the approach, as Calvus conducted me to the high brick *insula* where she lived, the leading lady, who laughs before the joke is over, the better to own the joker. Her levity was threat and invitation to whoever was near her, damn him. I could imagine the line of her throat, the lifted chin; it was naked, her silky laugh, defied touch. What slave girl laughed like that? Not little Melissa; no respectable matron either: my mother never. The owner of that laugh was someone to – what exactly? – *master*, dream of mastering, which conceded mastery. I had to hate her to have the nerve to play her, this before I had seen more of her than a fine hand, coming from inside the house, fingering the lucky door. I had betrayed her, gladly, with Ipsitilla, double-decked, I wanted her to know, before she was even aware that I existed.

The door widened, a cat's waking yawn; slim fingers shaped white intimation of imminent appearance. Then she stepped out, Clodia Metelli, *the* woman of Rome, queen of Metelli and Claudii, class incarnate, prize prize. Caelius watching, I made a so-so face. Arms that flowed like water, they said of Antiodemis, barbarian dancer who triumphed at Gaius Marius's triumph, whichever one it was, of six. The lady C. looked into the street as if she had caught the thud of my heart (no trite coin like that can be suffered to pass in a poem, but what appetite has an original register?). Desire was not the point; I wanted her attention, inquisitive "Hullo, who might you be?"

Tall? Short? A goddess has no measure, more an aura to look up to, and imagine pulling down. The hair, that hair, was brushed back in oil-dark curls from blanched forehead, naked temples; the lips bitten, I bet, to that ready pout; kohl-dark eyes outshone the sun. My ambition stood there and knew it, before she knew me, I her.

Caelius said, "Life in Rome is a dangerous art. *Nota bene*: genuine feelings play no part, not on the Palatine, not in politics, nor in love. Promise me you'll never make that mistake."

Would he have said it, had he not guessed it made already? They came out after her, her rhubarbing riot. I envied their proximity, lucky more than a few, privy to her mockery, soliciting laughs that never shrilled. I stood against some lover's rusty graffiti on the street corner as her people swept the flagstones for her. "*Amat qui scribit, pedicatur qui legit*" (He loves who writes this; who cons it can shove it).

"True love has no known address in Rome," Caelius said. "Never make that mistake."

I looked her up and down, as if I cared; and as if she did. I had betrayed her before we started, she me. The goddess was human, and not that tall. I stood there, craving the light lash of her indifference, prayed to the twin gods on the street corner to clink to my cause. Her feet were bigger than Eirene's.

"Be ready to hate her, G.V.C.; be ready not to give a damn." Caelius' forked tongue played the Pythian part. "Then make your move."

She and her crowd started down the street. The lady looked not at me but at the air beside me, as if it were a glass to check her coiled conceit. Then she twitched her head, that head, to confirm that they were there behind her, jostling johnnies, on her Argus-eyed tail. The hair in profile a soft bun, parody of matronly severity. Oh to let it down, and see her, dis/tressed, shake herself gladly younger!

"There you have her," Caelius said, "and if you do, you won't be the first, nor yet the last. *Suprème de* Bitch, the beauty! Mind the snap of her snatch if you venture your stiff tail anywhere near it. Madness follows. I advise cold baths. Picking, then not choosing, is all her style."

She was accustomed to company; her escort's dawdle, their leaning eagerness to please made her vivid face articulate; the puckered insinuation of her mouth, her left, my right, doubled intimacy with disdain. She was no longer amused; did that amuse her? Had someone whom she had hoped to spot, if only to ignore, failed to bring his tangent to her circle? I understood her, literally, shortened as I was by the gutter of the grooved street; its stepping stones granite buskins to pedestal unspattered ankles, toes immaculate from merchants' muck.

She gave the middle distance a glance, where I stood, twenty paces away, Caelius too. I smiled, more to myself than at her. I had already sketched her likeness, and liked it, work in progress. Was she looking at me, or at Red? Picking and not choosing was all her style. I scanned the scene for something more important to look at, then back at her, not focussing, as if she were an obstacle to what I was looking for. I pecked her with my eyes, in passing, read her displeased by my insolence; if only she'd noticed. She did, it seemed, and raised her hand, that hand.

"Caelius, heavenly to see you!" She parodied herself; for my pleasure and disappointment? I wished her grand and refused to care if she was, for which she had to be more than grand. "Who's this silky fellow," she said, "or is it sulky?"

"Gaius Valerius Catullus."

"Catullus?" she said.

"From Verona. His father's a friend of Julius, hence…"

"Verona," she said.

Did I catch a hint of interest in her trisyllabic spacing of a city never in regular regard? Might her hyphenated tone not promise that the game was on? Scorn for scorn, I proposed no less, no more.

"You haven't got a message for me possibly, have you, Veronese?"

"Of course," I said. "To be delivered in private or not at all."

"I scent trouble," she said. "My favourite fragrance. Are you coming with us to the theatre? The only place where we can find out what slaves really get up to and envy their licence."

I said "I'm promised elsewhere."

"Hotter tickets, are there? Where?"

"What are you up to?" Caelius said. "And why?"

"*Au rendezvous des Muses,*" I said, and turned to go lest I find myself sealed like Pirithous when he made his wanton pitch for Persephone or a witless Perseus by Rome's Medusa stoned. Antique references jostled for audition, fruit of Solonaki's chrestomathy.

"He's got his Cisalpine gall," I heard her say, "I'll give him that, if nothing else," and I smiled into the future. "Publius promised he'd be here."

Caelius said. "Explains why he isn't. That's the kind of sweetheart he is, your frater. Never the one he's promised to be."

"Are you looking for a radish, Red?"

"The riddle of the sphincter, not the stuff my dreams are made on, lady." Caelius earned an enviable laugh, low and loaded, it seemed, with availability for more. Oh to be the trigger for that pull!

As leaden feet took me on down towards the forum, I heard her call to her followers, at once peremptory and (she had to clear her throat) enchanting. "Come on, my dears, we're going to be late. They won't hold the play for us."

Caelius said, "They know you like to make an entrance that gets everybody up."

"Caelius…"

"The same."

"*Always* the same; your big mistake."

"*Semper* if seldom *fidelis*. Always rely on me, dear lady, if you want to be let down."

I was slighted by his unhesitating familiarity. What sweet revenge to displace him! When did desire have a single motive? Passion had better not be pure if it's to last: what love persists unsalted by the jealousy of those excluded from it? I walked away with a grateful grudge.

"Veronese did she call you?" The speaker was shorter than his voice; it gave him nice insolence, promised breeding. He might have been younger than me; his confidence was older.

I said, "My father's estate is not far from Verona. Sirmio."

"You're a Catullus."

"Gaius Valerius."

"And mean to be *the* Catullus, do I have you right?"

"I haven't thought about it."

"Marcus Juventius. My family is from near Verona. Might that ease the scowl from your handsome countenance?"

"Your two eyes are of different colours," I said.

"One says stop, the other go. Is madam Clo-clo a target of yours?"

"I'm not sure that I have targets," I said.

"I'm certain you do."

"Curiosities," I said. "I have those. In all sizes."

"And shapes?"

"Your father made a fortune with Cornelius Sulla, am I right?"

"Slaves. By the thousand. As yours did, if I'm right."

"And you do like to be."

"The trouble with the ladies," Juventius said, "is that it takes so damn long to bring them to the shticking point, do you not agree?"

"I hadn't thought about it, to tell you the truth."

"Why say it's the truth if it is? You're too pretty to have to worry, is that it?"

"There is no it. I told you: curiosity's the lure."

"Nice of you to lie to me, Gaius Valerius. Believe me, you have definite ambitions, but not yet decisive ones. Do I read you right? To make your mark, one way or another."

"Or both," I said.

"That's the nicest thing you've said to me so far."

"I had no mind to be nice."

"That's becoming; not altogether convincing. But then again, perhaps the mind's activities are overrated. You have an aura, Gaius V., a muskiness even, that gives you away before you have any call to sell yourself. You're a giver and a taker."

"You amuse yourself," I said.

"And leave you not entirely without a smile. You're not familiar with Rome, as I am sure you will be in time, so you read her ramparts as more...impregnable than they often are. You're not sure – correct me if I'm right – whether you are here to scold or to...qualify."

I said, "You're very expert in...presumption."

Juventius said. "I have in mind to kiss you for a while and have you not want me to, until you do, which you will."

"You must do a lot of this. You make it seem very easy."

"What better to do than amuse myself by amusing others? *Variatio* keeps me busy, Gaius, and remarkably happy, while I have my hair and my teeth. I recommend it to you. The point may come when I settle for crass cupidity and fatten the fortune my father was resigned to bequeathing to me. He knew I would make what he considered bad use of it, enough to live on, in style, and also – he was right in thinking – do little or less to fatten it. Perhaps if I marry, I shall learn to be commercial. You're afraid of something."

"Do I trust you?"

"Save that nonsense for the ladies," Juventius said. "One of us must make a start," he said. "If you want to be the girl, I shall have to be the boy, shall I not?"

Calvus was my tutor in Roman flyting. We sat in the patio of his little house on the Janiculum and traded conceits; ithyphallic red-cocked fountain gargling behind us, *sotto voce* prompter-prick.

> *"Yesterday, Licinius, was one to treasure!*
> *Improvising salty lines our pleasure,*
> *Keeping it light the rule, we rapped it.*
> *You chose a metre; I capped it,*
> *Back and forth, shooting a line,*
> *Lashing out jokes, ditto wine.*
> *Time came at last for me to quit,*
> *Roasted by your versatility and wit.*
> *My heat no wretched snack could calm*
> *Nor sleep my sorry eyes bring balm.*
> *All night, in heat, on my pallet bed*
> *Shagged out and pretty well half-dead,*
> *This poem, dear heart, in heat I penned*
> *To prove the grief you caused me, friend.*
> *Don't dare snub my solicitation*
> *Or slap me down, dear heart, with deprecation.*
> *Nemesis might come, claim a forfeit;*
> *She can be a bitch, so best come off it!"*

With Alexandrian mock intimacy, I signed it, *"peripsyma sou"*.

Marcus said, "I'm not alone. Do you want to join us? Oh my goodness, the face, Gaius Valerius, I love it. You seek pain like Actaeon."

"It sought him," I said.

"I you, you me," he said. "There's the comedy of it."

"And the tragedy?"

"Between us, I think not, unless you insist. The simplicity of it vexes the ladies, rarely the women. You kiss, Gaius Valerius, as if it mattered. That little gasp, like an entrance fee! That's your great charm; and, if you mean it, probably your even greater mistake."

As I walked back to the Suburra, three men came towards me from under a dark archway, quite as if they were waiting for me. One had a black eye-patch. Before I had time to run, they were past me. Fear became curiosity, and callousness. I watched as they attacked a solitary man who had just stepped from a house. His resistance was silent, brief and futile. They stabbed him with practised repetition, confirmed that he was dead and walked on, saying nothing and in no hurry.

A few days later, Calvus took me to a *soirée* at madam's house, leaving little Quintilia to her female friends; not *that* little, in truth: trust five-foot nothing to have a wife half a cubit taller; and trust Caelius to remark that Calvus loved her because he always put on an extra six inches when he was with her. Tonic charmer, the lady Q., who looked only at Gaius, he at her; none so uxorious, when Venus hooks him, as your once promiscuous *literatus*.

> *"No one in the world like him, you say,*
> *Dear Juventius, no gorgeouser George*
> *Than poppety from Pesaro (noted for its pox)?*
> *Bloodless is he as a gilded torso.*
> *Your heart is his? You'd daresay sooner him than me?*
> *'Know what you're doing,' say you? Do you?"*

There she was, Clodia; the profile, the nose, arms on alabaster show, the rest guesswork; and I quick to guess. I scowled, as she chose – it felt like a choice – to go on wasting herself on the grinning Egnatius, whom Calvus labelled Spick and Spaniard (his family made a packet trawling with Julius); already a betrayal! Provincial prude, I thought her divine; even the feet: was she wearing a smaller size? When she looked around to size the company, it was Calvus she lit on. I stood there sleeved in callow sweat, like Ares when he first saw Aphrodite and threw away his shield; she saw it, damn her, my shine.

I turned away, coaxed an attendant slave girl into collusive smiles. I would have her guess that I shared her longing, if she had one, for a different world. She pouted and screwed a finger into her cheek; meaning what? Ask a Neapolitan. Sauced, I thought to force her down, Circassian country cunt, one arm bracing her neck, dark forehead forced against the mosaic satyr who piped on the expensive floor, stuff her arse up, tussock of Asian hair in my grasp. She smiled, unsurprised, implying yes, of course. I did not want her yes; only the no she had no right to could spice her meat.

Clodius, pretty fellow, came towards me, face creamed with leftover laughter from something Calvus had said; about me, was it? Publius saw the girl I was conning, his sister's maid, put an angled arm around her, plucked the grape of her nipple; doing what I had not, because I had not. He weighed a buttock, let her go with a see-you-later squeeze; not a man to keep his hands in his toga and act the Olympian, Publius C., when he can operate so smartly with them. She glanced back at him, Lydian charmer, his low attention more commanding than my lofty sympathy; the bitch, the beast, oh to outdo them both!

"You look broody, Veronese. Sis denied you her attention, has she? No call to work the manly jaw. You're not the only one. Your silly ambition possibly?" He took my arm, fingered the muscle, as if I were that girl, my tit hers. "Come and talk to her. Gaius Calvus tells me you write wicked verses if people aren't nice to you."

"Can happen, even if they are."

"Sapphics a speciality, do I gather, girly?"

43

"*Variatio,*" I said, to try him.

"Never pinch the same tit twice, that your point, *pedantesco mio?*" He kissed me on the lips. "Here to guy us, Gaius, are you?" He shrilled in self-delight. "*And* oil us up? I know where that one came from. How's Juventius treating you these days? And his ingle?"

He walked quickly to Clodia Metelli and told her something that made her look at me, not quite as I expected, and then again at him. They leaned together and smiled, cheek by cheek, as if hooped in an amulet.

"Come and entertain her." He raised his voice with carrying shrillness. "My sister likes poets; preferably for breakfast."

"If they scan to my satisfaction."

"Poet and poetry," I said, "by no means the same article."

"It speaks," Publius said. "It pronounces! Wearing its cleverest clogs, however squeaky."

Clodia's expression relished and excused her brother's provocation. Publius was scanning the company. The quiver of her brow, above steady eyes, implied that she was sure I understood; humouring him, promising to be serious with me; so it amused me to think, at least.

"*Oikade,*" Calvus said. "I'm going home, Gaius."

"If I had Quintilia waiting for me, I'd do the same," I said.

"Next time," Clodia said. "Bring some of your work in progress, Greekling."

Clodius was smiling at me, as if he had instigated his sister's curiosity and I owed him something. Before I went to sleep that night, I concocted an antidote to their contagion.

> "*Lesbius her doll, Lesbia his duck.*
> *Veronese? Who the fuck?*
> *'Never one of us,' they shriek.*
> *Best known for their bloody cheek.*"

A few days later, I went to see her, omitting that squib from my toted samples. I told myself that I was heading for the Palatine only for the pleasure of shocking a rich and spoiled woman. I took care, however, in the choice I made to brighten my bouquet.

> "Here's a funny one for you, sweetheart,
> Lend me your ears, stand by for a giggle.
> If you love me, prove it, by laughing.
> Funnier than funny, this one.
> I came on a slave boy, humped on the job
> With his chick. Presuming open house,
> In I popped and, thanks to Cupid's nod,
> We were ox and ass, tandem at the plough."

"When did this happen?"

"Are you sure it did?"

"Anything else in your quiver?"

> "Ameana, that public amenity,
> Has sent me a final demand:
> Ten big ones! Her with her nose
> Like a pickle, the cash-strapped
> Formian's lady. Call her friends,
> And quickly, a posse of doctors too,
> The girl is far from sane, or else
> She'd look in the mirror
> And spot she's a busted flush."

"Aren't you nice," she said, "to be so nasty?"

"I should never have shown them to you."

"Naughty apple, polished for teacher, is it?"

"Work in progress was what you asked for."

"Well, mind you work on it."

I scowled; and when she smiled, smiled not. Was she older, closer? I looked again at my verses; and found no fault in with them. She moved a questing finger and then withdrew it, *dulce ridens*, worldly charmer.

"You like to be cruel," she said.

"When it scans sweetly, who doesn't rate the snap of conclusive jaws?"

Her frown conceded justice, and promised it; she could not be shocked, but she could be bored, it told me; had better not be. We each entertained the other and played at meaning it, whatever it was.

"You haven't actually sent it to her, have you, *la poveretta*?"

"When I wrote it exclusively to amuse you?"

"Why go to girls like…Ameana?"

"If not to her, to whom? The names, the names!"

"You certainly can get grammatical when roused."

"And you? Charm and sarcasm in the same *salsa*."

"Have you written about me and kept it up your sleeve?"

"I don't stretch to flattery," I said. "And in your case, flattery is all that would truly serve. My sleeves are full of other things."

She said, "Wait till you know me better. Come again. Flash some of your more daring wares. So far so tame, wouldn't you agree?"

I left her for a few days and then took her another garnished *pot pourri*.

> "Here's a funny one, sweetheart, a cracker;
> Lend me your ears, prepare for a giggle.
> If you love me, prove it…and laugh.
> Funnier than funny, this one.
> I surprised a slave boy, humped on the job
> His girl an open invitation, pari passu,
> In I dropped; thanks to the mother of Love,
> And shared the hard work with him."

Those eyes remained unblinking. Was she shocked? Did it amuse her to have me fear so, or wish it? It was not what people had led me to expect. I scowled at her failure to smile, which all but brought her to do so. I read her to be relishing duplicity, hers and mine, the trouble each was taking, and changed the register:

"Egnatius has got white teeth;
And flashes them everywhere.
Big case. Counsel winding up,
Jury in tears. E.'s grinning, ear to ear.
A cremation; only son, a paragon;
Weeping mother, inconsolable.
E's grinning, ear to ear. Always!
Never mind what, when, where,
He flashes. Gods, how he flashes!
It's sick; he thinks it's smart.
He thinks it's Rome; it's not.
Somebody should tell him? Let me!
Sonny, suppose you belonged here,
Or were Sabine, or Tiburtine,
Raw Umbrian, Etruscan lardo,
Hillbilly Lanuvian (spade face,
donkey teeth), or from over the Po,
One of us, as they say, suppose you were
Anybody who cleaned his teeth au point…
I'd still say no, no; no flashing, flash man.
What's more off-putting than a put-on grin?
But, señorito, you're a Dago, and we know
In Dagoland you make your piss
A home-made dentrifrice,
Gargle to ginger the gingiva.
So: the spicker his span by day,
The more E's pissed the previous night.
Cheese?"

She scowled. "You total shit sometimes, aren't you? Poor old Eggnog!"

For a moment, it appeared she meant it; then she was laughing, and laughing; not *dulce* but *ridens*, nicely spaced, frowns for punctuation, as if she wanted to stop, but couldn't. She dried her eyes, straightened her face; and then she was laughing again. She tried to put on a scowl and was funny herself.

"If you ever put me in a poem..."

"Will be the day you live forever."

"And use my name, I was going to say, he'll kill both of us."

"Us," I said.

"You've heard about about the Metelli."

"But not about us," I said.

"I mean it."

"'No man,' she means, 'she'd marry before me,
Not Juppiter himself, on his knees;
Or she says, as women do,
Doodling on the wind, carving water!'"

"You carry those things with you, I'll bet, like small change. I said nothing of the kind."

"And I shall hold you to it."

She reached a hand for me, as if I were further from her than I was.

"I love you," I said, quite as if she had.

"Sounds like an accusation," she said, "As for you...I ought to hate you probably; if not fear you."

"That sounds promising," I said.

She looked towards the doorway, as if, having done nothing, we had done something. Conspirators in conspiracy without substance, our secret's sole ingredient was its secrecy. Nothing to hide was already something. There was a measure of danger even from Fausta for all their cheek-to-cheek boudoir giggles. She was a shining Numidian girl, full-lipped, devoted to her mistress, save that she belonged to Celer. When, decidedly alone, I dared to tell Clodia that I truly loved her, she laughed; so did I, as if I hadn't meant it. Had I not?

"On the assumption," she said, "that you don't mean a word, bring me some more of your doodles."

"Do I get kissed in return?"

"*Quid pro quo*," she said. "Mark of the mercantile!"

"No man, she tells me, she'd marry before me,
Not if Jupiter himself were on his knees;
Or so she tells me. As women do to men in love.
She doodles on the wind and runaway water!"

"I never told you anything of the kind," she said.

"And I shall hold you to it."

She said, "Come here."

I kissed those lips, hard, as if she had not proposed them.

"I meant every word," I said.

"Every *other* word," she said, softening. "I recognise stepping stones when I see them."

"If you were not married…"

"You'd have nothing to offer me; nor occasion to offer it. You'd never get near me, or wish to. As it is, I'm one of those women…"

"Who leaves all the stales in the sand." I could taste her blood, unless it was mine.

"What did Calvus say about me? Talkative little runt with a remarkably large…vocabulary."

"How beautiful he rated you back in the days when he sent you his verses."

"*Pelted* me, more like it. And now? Nothing like true love to render a man prosaic."

"Expect me to turn turgid any second."

"What's she like, his *inamorata*?"

"He loves her, she loves him. If you and I were married…."

"You'd be looking elsewhere for your next gasp of applause."

"You don't love him, do you, your husband?"

"This is Rome," she said. "Baucis and Philemon have no known address here."

"I do rate flash allusions."

"I know you do. Why else flash them?"

"Give me leave and I'll take you out of…your house…"

"My *husband's* house. And then where should I be? It's part of my...charm. Confess it, you came to see the sorceress in her lair."

"Circe, some people call you."

"Caelius the first. Don't deny it."

"How else shall I get you to believe it?"

"Careful!" she said. "Quick on cue every time smacks of glibness. I learnt that from Roscius. A clever man makes a woman smile by being unhurried and then... delivering. It promises the expertise that marks the expert tease."

"Damn Roscius. I had that ready and I was waiting to say it."

"If you want another kiss," she said, "or two, by way of consolation prize...." She prompted me with a dart of her tongue.

"Damn consolation." My bold hand surprised her. "How many have there been, before me?"

"And how many of you are there, Veronese? And what makes you think there's you?"

"Imagine if we stopped pretending and said what we truly wanted to say."

She looked at me. Was the leading lady honouring Roscius, the clever silence? Her eyes made keen fun of me; silence her line, my cue.

"Or, preferably, doing," I said, weakening first; or having her think so.

Her lip moved, but uttered nothing, until she cleared her throat – that throat! – and said, with a neat little cough, "I was...I was brought up to pretend."

"Are you going to tell me more? Do. Everything."

"More is one thing; everything too much."

"Pretend what?"

"Not to...mind. The use they made of me. I was betrothed, as the nice people used to say, when I was twelve years old. Betrothed as in thrown to the..."

"I know: Metelli. They do seem to recur when...what happened to you exactly?"

"To my father," she said. "My...exemplary father."

"Who exemplified what exactly?"

"Folly...as in declining when asked to join the killing party. Claudians are too proud to double as executioners. They leave that to swarthies in red caps. My father had a choice with no choice: exile and penury or else. Because he wasn't prepared to play killer for blotchy. Lucius Cornelius had this red hot map of Asia burning on the side of his face. Even now he's dead, people are still just a little afraid to call him what he was."

"Which was what?"

"Murderer." She looked at me like an enemy. "Provincials were lucky, sitting on rural fences. They missed the cut. When my father needed a way back into society, I was his...ticket. They banged me down to a Metellus I never met until the day...and the night. *Hymen Hymenaeus.* How did it go? Not with a bang."

"Whom you now punish by...teasing others."

"Are you being teased? Or am I giving you licence?"

"Both?"

"You've yet to decide, isn't it? What you want of me. Or what you'll do to get it."

"Two faces are better than one; especially when both are yours."

"I think I liked you better a minute ago."

"Let's go back," I said. "I'll find another line."

"You write like a tiger..."

"Hyrcan, I trust."

"...pay court like a boy, pout like a baby, compose like...no one else in the world." It was an accusation until it grew its laurel: she laughed again, then stopped herself. "One day you'll do as much to me."

"Never," I said. Then: "More!"

"You had to say."

Word came that Celer was on his way to the house. I stubbed my toe on the threshold as I left, less afraid to meet him than wishing that I had reason for such fear. Success and pleasure would be identical if I had been whispering in her ear and had her throw back her head, stretch the throat, produce – by my attempted kiss, the try that parodies itself – those cadences of golden contempt, then check them with the pleasure

I forced upon her, fingers plying her bevelled nest.

I sat and scratched a poem in the patio of Julius's pad.

> *"We can live, Lesbia mine, and love and love.*
> *People will talk? Greybeard elders*
> *With edifying moral strictures?*
> *How about they work them up their asses?*
> *Suns can set, and suns can rise again;*
> *For me and you, once our brief light goes out,*
> *Night forever; sleep beyond reprieve.*
> *Give me a thousand kisses, then a hundred,*
> *Then a thousand more and add a hundred;*
> *Then all our thousands thousanded*
> *Will jumble the figures, wreck the reckoning,*
> *So no knowing sour puss can hiss us*
> *Or slap a tax on uncountable kisses."*

"Sign of the second-rate," Aurelius announced, in a voice pitched to be overheard, "don't you agree, Furius, parading self-serving sentiments?"

"Calling her Lesbia whoever she is tells us more than he knows, don't you think so? *Much.*"

"Or is it *she* knows? Pretty indecent his stuff, don't you agree?"

"He could very well be one of *them*, my dear; quite the Greekling, so they tell me, Master C. One of the lacier Daimonians, why not? If he ends up jumping off a cliff, like his treasured Sappho, never say you wasn't warned."

"Some people will do anything to make a splash."

Calvus came up to me, "I shouldn't publish that one if I were you," he said.

"Good as that, is it? Very nice of you to say so."

Those Roman knuckles, just under my the shoulder, was the best smile he could manage.

"Pedicabo vos atque irrumabo.
Bugger you and likewise sucks,
Aurelius who stoops, Furius who stabs.
So you 'conclude' from my little verses,
Which, granted, can be 'pretty indecent'
That I am pretty and indecent too.
Yes, proper poets should be dedicated;
The work's another thing entirely;
It gives a man's lines spice and flavour
To be juicy and not entirely naice,
That's how to give readers a lift.
The young need no leavening prods,
But greybeard sods with ponderous kit,
Who don't find it easy to rise.
So you've read of my thousands of kisses,
And you call me less than a man
Well, bugger you, as hinted above,
And when that's over, sucks!"

She sipped fresh air, shifted in her chair, a tiny slide forward exciting new folds, continued to look at me, as if there might be more. I kissed the twitch of humour on her lips, took her sigh for invitation; she mine for impatience. She eyed my frustration, blinked her own. A louder sigh elicited her servant girl, reminder that we were never alone, threat that we might never be. Lesbia read the message that Fausta had brought, smiled a smile that said "later", and put the tablet aside.

I said, "I can't go on like this."

"Of course you can't, and of course you will. I've done as much for years."

"Beware the plural, it cackles like Capitoline geese, and gives your show away. Your husband, does he suspect...?"

"About you? What is there to suspect?"

"That's your pleasure, dare I guess? Hiding that you have nothing to hide?"

"My pleasure is the look on your face, as if I owed you something, when I don't – and you know it – owe you a thing."

"Do you not want me to come here?"

"Unless you want to, you certainly shouldn't. When shall I see you again?"

How many times did he walk through the forum and up, thinking it should be the last? How often did he dawdle, consent to talk to this man or that, from the audience of the previous night's recital, wanting a copy, a bookseller promising fame, in Greek, if the gentleman had the money? He did not need to go up the shiny slope, past incoming pigs and sheep, tight tide, boxed rabbits, caged pollies, taking note of what did not matter to him, vintners with streaked barrels, carters hauling creaking stone and timber; but up, eventually, he went. How often did he get there and wait, shrug, go in, as if bold? How many other things did he do, with whom?

> *"I filched a kiss, when you were fooling,*
> *Juventius my honey, sweeter than ambrosia;*
> *And paid the felon's price: an hour or more*
> *Nailed to the cross, I'll not forget it.*
> *No excuses, mercy pleas, no snivels*
> *Commuted malevolence one bit.*
> *Next second, you dashed pretty lips*
> *With gouts of water, a backhander*
> *Purged them of the taste of me,*
> *Neat as a poxy, piss-faced whore*
> *Poor me, delivered to pitiless love,*
> *Tortured with exquisite refinement;*
> *It didn't stop: my ambrosial kiss*
> *Turned sadder than sad old hellebore.*
> *Is that how you pay a luckless lover back?*
> *Never again a kiss of yours will I filch."*

*What did Metellus say to him, if he did more than nod; with what eyes
did the consul regard the callow poet, the poet the consul?*

"He's your excuse, isn't he, *o kirios sou*, for not doing what you want?"

"What you want me to want, might that be?"

"Do you not? You do unless…this is what you always do. Which I
am promised."

"If you love me, why do you want to hurt me?"

"Can I hurt you? That might be why."

"What choice do I have, Veronese? The Metelli take things badly,
you know that."

"When there is nothing to find?"

"They can still be found. He could kill us both."

"For sitting here."

She said, "For looking like doing what you want."

I said, "And you not?"

"Not here," she said, "not ever."

"What if I find somewhere?"

"While Celer's in Rome? Not possible."

"But when he goes….wherever consuls have to go?"

"You'll need a friend you can trust and I can. Not to tell anyone even
that we trust him. Not easy to find. Nothing runs faster than rumour."

"Meanwhile?"

> *"Myself and the one I fancy, Aurelius,*
> *I put you under notice,*
> *Grant this modest favour;*
> *If ever you could rise*
> *To keeping one thing sweet*
> *(Roughly, pollution-free)*
> *Keep this young person so for me.*
> *I don't mean just from the plebs –*
> *They don't bother me too much.*
> *A woman's when the sales are on,*

No time to mix pleasure with business.
Quite frankly, it's you that I fear,
Prick with a hard reputation;
You've got it in for all the boys.
Keep it up, that's fine by me,
Wherever, whoever you fancy,
As long as it's not around here.
Look, one simple exception,
How big a concession is that?
So...if you get any nasty ideas,
You sod, and dare to get cracking
(Tempting that sweet head into your noose),
A solemn warning, buddy boy:
You'll wish you'd had a different end.
I'll lash you up with the hatch wide open
And stuff the back passage with fish
Mullet spiked with radicchi,
Prescribed suppository."

Had I made promises to Lesbia? Had she to me? What we had between us, our...*amicitia* I liked to think, was unique between a man and a woman, but who said it was exclusive? Life went on. I took it as I found it or it found me.

I walked out of Celer's house, past the unseeing orbs of ancestral sentinels, stiff guardians of his rich hall, and was several yards down the street before he and his retinue became important as they turned the corner and made it his. I played the dreamer, as if drilling an unaligned army of words in my capital playground; not a phrase to greet the Consul with, who took the city literally to be his. I allowed him not to see me, by seeming not to see him.

"Young Catullus."

I played surprised. "Good afternoon, sir."

"Mooning at my lady's closed door, are you? Half the men in Rome are in the same case. Makes us laugh, she and I."

"I am glad to hear that something does, *domine.*"

"You've heard about the Metelli and their short temper."

"And shorter shrift," I said. "Of course. Why?"

His flat lips promised no reprieve. "Allow me to make a suggestion."

"Allow me to be grateful that you might do so."

"Yes, yes," he said. "It's this: if I can raise a favourable wind, which with Gnaeus Pompeius' help I almost certainly can…"

"Boreas itself bends at his command, they say."

"Boreas, does he? How about if you were to join my staff? It might be…politic. And keep you out of…mischief. My wife, I'm sure, will be of the same opinion."

I had been warned. It was quite encouraging.

> "*Lesbia, when her old man's on the scene,*
> *Can't put me down enough, he thinks it*
> *Fwightfully funny; brainless ass!*
> *If I wasn't on her mind, she'd have nothing*
> *To keep quiet about. But bitch, bitch, bitch,*
> *Proves I am, and – here's the clincher –*
> *She's sore: the hots! Ergo, talk, talk, talk!*"

"Here's another one you can try for size, *cara.* Early number:

> "*Catullus, Catully, quit playing the fool.*
> *What you guess is over, tell yourself let it go,*
> *Yes, a thousand suns once blazed full upon you,*
> *You came and came again, often as she whistled,*
> *The darling; never to be loved that much again.*
> *In those days, you had a host of giggles.*
> *When you said please, her noes were yeses;*
> *And how they blazed on you, those thousand suns.*
> *Now she wants no more; so don't do what you can't.*
> *She's cut and run? Don't play the sadster.*
> *Cheers then, kid. Catullus the hard case,*

Ain't coming back, don't want what doesn't want him.
You'll be sorry when no one's on his knees,
Bitch. So go to hell, how's it feeling now?
Who'll come calling you beautiful or mean it?
Whom will you have to love, or own you're his?
Who'll do the kisses then, whose lips your meat?
Game over, Catully; stick with it: stop!"

She said, "What's her name? This tail you were writing about?"

I said, "One of our domestics, father's. I imagined loving her. Melissa. Or was it Eirene? I only know I loved her and I also..."

"...wanted to punish her, see her punished; but not by you. You'd sooner watch, and shiver with her stripes. You shake your head; meaning I'm right?"

"Your eyes," I said, "they're so dark and so..."

"So what?" she said. "Find a description I haven't heard. Nothing to do with lakes; and skip mythology."

"Lambent."

"*Lambent?* Nobody *says* lambent. Proves what I've always suspected: you're never really talking to me, little Gaius; you're lapping me in words like a mummy. All the time you're with me, you're also against me."

"Love and war, Janus pair."

"Beware the Metelli, Gaius Valerius; remember what happened to Naevius."

"Old hat," I said, "please don't push that one on me, feathered or not. That was then."

"In Rome then is never far away. Especially when it comes to dealing with poets, both uppity and puppety. Do you like shopping at all?"

"Shopping?"

"I need a pet. Do you know Vettius?"

"Vettius. The only Vettius I know about is the one Marcus Tullius talked about re Verres: fell in love with a young slave girl, didn't he, in Capua...?"

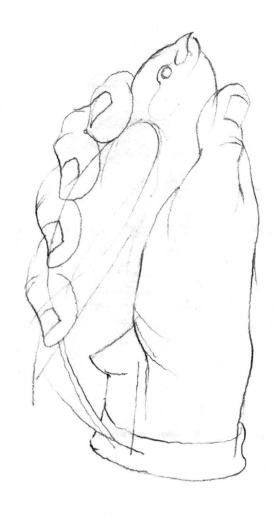

"And tried to turn the world upside down, but the world did it to him instead. It's always liable to do that. To women especially."

"The world has all the luck," I said.

"The Vettius I'm talking about claimed in some detail that he'd..."

"...had the pleasure? And had he?"

She said, "A radish taught him otherwise."

"A radish?" I said. "Taught him what?

"Two spiky ones. They taught the cheeky Master V. the Greek for love, just where it hurts the most. Be warned."

"Your chaps?"

"My working stiffs," she said.

"I can do stiffer for you than they ever will; I promise."

> *"To you, if to anyone, Vettius, you shit,*
> *Can be said what's commonly said to long-winded poops.*
> *A tongue like yours, given the opening, could get a job*
> *Licking arses or toe-jam from peasants' sandals.*
> *You wish we'd all jolly well get lost?*
> *Only open your mouth; you'll jolly well get your wish."*

"I'm thinking of a little bird," she said. "In the pet department. One that'll fit sweetly in my hand and be my...comforter. Where can I find one of those?"

I put my hand up. "My love is only for you, Lesbia *mou*. How's that for comfort?"

"I don't ever want to hear anyone else calling me that. Lesbia. I'll know you blabbed."

"Your secret is mine. And the Muse's, whom no one can vouch for."

"Trust you to keep your word like a Cretan!"

"And trust you to rely on it, *kallistê mou*."

She savoured that, the smile she withheld the sweeter for its twitched denial. "I wish I could go down to the forum, and part the waves as if I had Celer's lictors with me. Why are you smiling? You thought of something. I bet it wasn't nice."

"Godlike he seems
Or – blasphemy is it? – higher yet,
Who sits with her, one to one, who hears
Her sweetly laugh the laugh
That scores my sorry senses.
I had but to see you, Lesbia, and...
What's to be said when speechless?
Tongue knotted, flame threading
My limbs, ears ringing
With their own beat, eyes hooded,
Both, with bright night.
Idle time, Catullus? Dangerous that!
It makes you jumpy, up to this, up to that.
Spare time! Been known to humble kings,
Breach careless towns!"

"Was that not nice?"

"You are the one and only, aren't you?" she said. "Sometimes."

"'twere better if another said it,' as Tully's always saying."

"In the sweet talk department."

"But when do we march," I said, "is that what you mean?"

"I love it," she said. "But march...? I lack the boots."

"Never the spurs!"

Her foot was in my hand, the left, her chin in the air.

"Caged," she said, "the two of us."

'My dear Catullus, I hope that I can be forgiven for writing to a young poet whom I have never met formally. I know only that you are exceptionally fluent and witty. I find entirely understandable that you are inclined to the Greek style. As you may know, I spent time studying rhetoric in Rhodos under Posidonius. Greek arts are as dear to me as to you. This letter seeks not to dispose you to abandon the source of so many of your stylistic ingenuities but rather – let me come to the heart of the matter – not to emigrate, *pour ainsi dire*, when it comes to attitudes. I know better than to write to you in order to talk about myself, but – as you may have heard, in the circles you seem to favour – there is a movement afoot to indict me for what I do to save our country from L. Sergius Catilina, a neoterist in the worst possible, revolutionary sense. What I did was authorised, if not demanded, by the overwhelming majority of senators.

'It would be agreeable to claim that your friend Caesar's dissent from that majority was motivated only by patriotic piety, but that young man (as I still think of him) is in a great hurry for greatness, if undecided how best to procure it by legitimate means. His plans to expand our provinces on the far side of the Alps have at least as much to do with remedying his own financial situation as with adding lustre, and revenue, to the republic. I too find Julius delightful company; who does not? But his impatience to prevail threatens the serenity of the republic, if never as insolently as the unpretty Publius Clodius pilchard, who has singled me out as the target for his vitriol, not because of the principles which he claims to be honouring but because I stand for the responsible public service which he is pleased to deride. You will have heard how he went on active service and found it honourable to incite the soldiers to mutiny. Your innovations in verse, my dear young friend (I hope I may call you that), are one thing, his in conduct and politics quite another. I do not for a moment suspect you of sharing his vices, but I ask you, because of the admiration you excite and deserve, to seek a wider audience for your virtuoso qualities than may be found in his coterie. If I may be excused, as a man of some small literary experience, for playing the pedagogue, there is more to be said for our traditional Latin style and posture, including a certain seriousness, than your present practice seems to salute.

'My friend Titus Lucretius Carus is proving, I believe, that our hexameter (whatever it owes to Homeric or Rhodian precedent) can be a sufficient tool for the declaration even of, let us say, unconventional views. Titus acknowledges, I grant you, of course, that his work is inspired by Epicurus ("*Primum Graius homo*", how chasteningly often that is true!) but – and the adversative has a rightful place here! – *De rerum natura* is composed *more Romano,* in a language which adds to the solemnity of his message, whether or not one cares wholly to embrace it.

'I am averse to writing about myself in the same breath, but I find some solace, despite the malice with which I am assailed, in the composition of verses which pay proper homage to – how else should they seek to surpass? – the fundamentally Roman style of Quintus Ennius, himself, as I need scarcely tell a precocious scholar such as yourself, rooted in Hellas by both blood and blood's corrective: our Latin *sérieux.* Forgive the jest, which proves only how much in earnest I am.

'I should consider it an honour should you have time to come to my house on the Palatine and cast a critical, if as I hope appreciative, eye on the modest account I am composing, in meta-Ennian style, of the days in which, as men of good will were quick to agree, I was acclaimed for saving for the republic from the depredations of Catiline and his adventurous friends, not a few of whom I had previously taken to be my own. It is unwise, when in Rome, to think that friendship can survive when polite forms are trodden under foot. It is sometimes right and necessary to pull back from *amicitia* (a favourite topic of my own) with people who are likely, in some cases certain, to lead you into a quagmire, from which they will be quicker to extract themselves than those whom they have seduced and will be happy to abandon.

'Yes, I am thinking of Publius Clodius and his associates, but also – and I trust you will forgive me – of the charms, as no one can deny, of his married sister, whose reputation is as lurid as she may choose to deny. I am not a man to confuse one thing with another, but there is a danger – why else should I take time out to compose this short letter? – that the lure of innovation, when it comes to verses, will dispose you to an eventually ruinous relish both for low topics and, however graced by great names, low company. As your admirer and a man of tastes not wholly dissimilar from your own, as a fellow-poet even, as I hope your reading of some of my work will allow me to call myself, I beg you to recur to honest associates and, for the future of your compositions, to themes worthy of your genius, for instance, and I mean it to be nothing but an indication, the *res gestae* of those who have chosen to preserve the republic and its finest traditions rather than to parade their vanities by reckless words and, as I fear we shall see, deeds which may at first be popular but must lead, as in Catiline's case, to personal ruin and public obloquy.

'If your verses are no more than clever squibs or cries of ecstasy, which will, I fear, turn to rage, as your innocence is betrayed, as it surely will be, if you go on as I fear you may, what chance do you have of being read, as Calvus surely will be, by future generations? Be a Roman poet, find exemplary themes and celebrate them without the cynicism which is the worst of all Greek spices, one which, with all its faults, you will never find in the thought or conduct of your humble correspondent. Allow me to advise you to renounce certain *salons* and find some public office, be it never so humble, in which to distinguish yourself and rise in circles where, if I am any judge, you will find a ready welcome. Do not – let me put it more clearly than tactfully – waste your substance on marginal subjects and dubious indulgence.'

"Jealousy in the form of homily. Not unusual that."

She said, "He's right though, isn't he?"

"I have little taste for the homiletic."

"Must you mount your highest horse to tell me so? With all those bossy vertebrae! Insolence rehearsed is cowardice in bronze."

"If that scanned, I'd steal it. Marcus T. is too prosaic to have any idea of what gives a poet his keenest appetite. Golden fruits are the only ones worth going out of one's way for."

"What if there's a dragon guarding the tree?"

"The dragon is part of the lure, if not the fruit."

"You're quite the Attic," she said, "when it comes to caps that fit. You should write plays. Roscius is always looking for new material to squint at."

"And then get hammered home in the same old way."

"I'm the Rubicon, Gaius V.," she said. "Once across me, there's no going back."

"And who would choose to?"

"Beware the dragon that guards the golden fruit."

"Without the dragon, how should they be gilded?"

"Kissing and telling," she said, in a Roman voice, "that's what poets do. And seldom wait long. The thing itself is never enough. Scribblers are not to be trusted, especially when it comes to older, married women."

"I will never say anything about you that you would wish otherwise."

"The opposite would be an easier promise to keep."

"I swear to you –"

"Don't scratch your vocabulary, Gaius Valerius, to flush out the most recherché gods you can think of."

"Idaean Dactyls don't impress you, the cleverest fingers?"

"The telling is better than the kissing, and the kissing for what can be told about it later. But not before, if you're wise."

"Are we going shopping for this pet of yours? Or shall I cheep for you, coo in your bosom like Venus's darlingest dove?"

"How can I be seen alone in public with a pretty provincial without a single consul dangling on his family tree? And you can't stay here much longer unless your hands learn how to behave."

I said, "Tell me something. Is it true –"

"Most things are, if we'd sooner they weren't."

"-about your brother dressing up as a Vestal Virgin and lighting a candle *chez* Julius C.?"

"Let's not chomp on reheated cabbage. I imagine he had a bet about it with someone. Ask your friend Julius, alias our revered Pontifex Max., if you've got the nerve."

I said, "How about topping him, your bro? What if I were to take you shopping as my likely little lad? In broad daylight. Put on an Asiatic cloak, borrow a servile hat and we can go down to the market and play...Fabius and Aurelius, well-known double act."

She said, "You like theatricals, don't you?"

"No more than you. You were on your impatient way to the theatre the first time I saw you. *Ela, koritsaki mou, pameh...*"

"You're bolder when you're not being yourself."

"Isn't that what education's for? Get the drag on, sonny boy."

She clapped for Fausta, looking at me, and was happy to whisper to her.

We stepped out of the street door, master, boy.

> *"Honey-sweet your eyes, Juventius,*
> *My dear! Just grant me leave to kiss them,*
> *Up to a thousand times…times three hundred!*
> *I'm never going to look as if I've had enough,*
> *Not if thicker than stiff-standing wheat*
> *Our harvest of futationes."*

"Oh, sir, you're overdoing it. In public too." Then in another voice, she said, "Fucking Juventius, am I?"

"Are you not?" I had to kiss the bitch, and did.

"What do men do," she said, "when they do those things?"

"Improvise," I said. The part for the hole."

"Your speciality."

"I love you, that's my sole speciality."

"Do you imagine doing to me what you do with him?"

"Or is it he with me? Not your place to ask, my pretty."

"Wish you could be a bully and a beast, don't you?"

"Roman citizens are born to tup the world."

I walked her past the senate house, hoping somewhat that we should be seen and not recognised, to sweeten the sweetness, as imposture, life's double-act, does. We passed the steep steps and the empty *rostra* and came past the snack dealers and booksellers to where Syrian merchants offered their cheeping parade of ladies' pets.

"Tell me, fellow, what kind of a bird do you call that one?"

"Golden finch, sir. Very uncommon."

"Looks uncommonly like a common sparrow to me. What do you say, Juvy? Will it do for madam what madam wants it to, do you suppose?"

"It looks very...dinky, sir," she said.

"Yours for a thou, *domine*," the man said.

"Does she care for dinky-dos, our lady?"

"You know her better than I ever will, *domine*." She squeezed my arm and stood close against me.

"If she gives me a hard time, I shall blame you, sonny."

"A hard time you should thank me for."

"Careful how you talk to me Unless you're careful I'll hail a red cap and have him give you six on your rosy little bum."

"You wouldn't do that to me, sir." She was tighter against me, one hand down, the other holding mine.

"Five hundred esses for you, senator, the little sweetheart. Final offer."

I said, "Three," for the pleasure of her double squeeze.

"Done," he said.

We turned away, the bird dangling between us in a wattle cage. "Now you'll love it more than you do me."

"Walk me around some more," she said. "You were right: it feels like freedom, slavery."

"When you're not a slave it does. I'd like to take you somewhere where no one can ever find us and love and love you forever."

"Then do it, big shot," she said. "If it's only one for night. You talk too much about what could be yours for the taking."

I looked at her, the boy.

Veranius, back from Spain, tanned as a hide, was saying hullo to Aurelius, and waved to me to join them. Clodia came obediently, bird against her breast, arm angled like a Theban terracotta Aphrodite (my father imported them, by the gross). I embraced the two travellers and said, "Any idea where I could take my going piece for a night or two?"

"Who is she, Gaius?"

"That'd be telling."

"i.e. married."

"All right, this one's mistress, if you must know."

"That who the bird's for?"

"Who else?"

"And where are you from, sonny?"

Clodia offered a clever frown. I said, "Pontus. It doesn't understand when you talk quickly."

"But takes the shaft like a well-oiled bitch, am I right?"

"In an emergency," I said.

"I have one of those," Aurelius said, "just looking at him, a big one, just under here. Leave this little number with me, Gaius, why don't you, while you're otherwise engaged? I'll add a few choice words to its vocabulary, not to mention choicer pleasures. What's Pontic for bottom up, open wide, and I'll thumb it in softly?"

The hooped bird cheeped my cue. "We must get this home to madam before this little lad gets into trouble."

Aurelius called back, "Your Rufa number's a beauty. Ruffian's out to get you unless Titus Menenius gets to him first."

"What's your Rufa number?" she said, when they were gone.

"Not for your ears," I said.

"After what you just prompted them to say, what's left? I want to hear it."

> "Rufa's a cocksucker; Rufulus her meat
> Bolognese style (alias signora Menenius),
> Spot her on the beat most days
> Around the graveyards, scoffing baked meats
> As they humble from funeral pyres.
> Gets her jollies from the crematorium johnny
> What don't even shave for the job."

I recited in an angry hurry, as if it were a concession I did not want to make. She laughed against my chest, looked up, unsmiling eyes.

"Bit tame," she said.

"All right," I said, "I have one for sonny boy as well:

"Aurelius, daddy of all the appetites
Today, yesterday, tomorrow, come what may,
The one I love, you fancy. Don't exactly hide it, do you?
You're one big giggle, and in public too:
So that's what's meant by sticking to it!
Gobbling sod, never miss a trick do you?
Imagine you can take my place?
I'll have you first, so sucks to you.
If you'd acted from fullness of heart,
I'd have no objection. As it is, I fear
Your appetites, in meat and drink,
Might infect my darling. Here's my advice:
Be sensible, lay off, have second thoughts.
Or get a proper mouthful."

"What's all that about exactly? Been bumping daisies with sunshine, have you?"

"If that prize bitch Clodia Metelli would let me love her as I want, be with me as I want, I should be a different man."

"Write her a poem to that effect, why don't you?"

"And have her laugh the laugh that launched a thousand quips?"

"To hell with the bitch. Do your stuff."

"Most skilful in speaking of Romulus' breed,
Many as there have been, Marcus Tullius,
And will ever be, throughout posterity,
The greatest possible thanks from Catullus.
As much the worst poet of all there are
As you the best of all who patrol the courts."

"What brought that one on? Tully'll it read as a straight tribute, you know that, don't you?"

"And is it not?"

"What did he say to bring you out in what sounds like a rash of compliments?"

"Depends on the reading. He wants me to be more…patriotic in my compositions."

"He warned you off the Clodii, didn't he, and this one in particular? Deny it and I'll know I'm right."

"And if I say you're right? Remember the Cretan."

"Go pedicate the Cretan," she said, "if that's your pleasure."

"I've written a reply," I said. "If you care to hear it."

"Men think what they say to each other is so important."

"Listen," I said, "and find out what I think of him."

> *"Vivamus atque amemus, me Lesbia…*
> *We should live, my Lesbia, and love.*
> *People are talking? So what?*
> *Let them whisper, moralising poops.*
> *Not worth a penny a dozen.*
> *Suns fall; suns come up again.*
> *But once our lights are out,*
> *It's one long sleep, forever, no reprieve.*
> *So give me a thousand kisses, a hundred more,*
> *Thousands on thousands, then, all count confounded,*
> *How can bad mouths tax uncountable kisses?"*

"She's scared of her husband," she said.

"That's not the story I've heard. Stories. I'm sure you know them."

"There was a difference."

"Which was what?"

"She didn't love them," she said, "did she? She was always hoping they'd say something she hadn't heard before."

"And how many did? The names, the names!"

"Don't worry," she said. "Romans don't rate originality. Their stones are rolled in the moss *maiorum*. Then again, she doesn't trust you…"

"To do what?"

"*Not do*. Turn her into one of the twists in one of your kaka stories."

"If she loved me she wouldn't calculate. I'd take her somewhere where no one would ever find us. As it is, she'll love this damn bird more than she will me. It'll certainly get closer to her than I ever can, the cow."

"You mustn't pout, master, or I'll lose respect for you." She/he reached up and kissed me and did not mind doing it again. "You know what you'd do, if you really wanted her? Find somewhere you can be alone, house belonging to someone you can trust. Wait till that husband of hers is out of town. Then don't ask her, tell her: to put a big cloak around herself and walk out of her house without anyone knowing or caring. She'll do it, bet you, if you...make the arrangements."

"I don't want her to do anything that might..."

"...put you at risk, isn't it?"

"Remember who you are, sonny boy, before I get those red-caps to redden you. Anything she'd blame me for."

"She blames you now. For waiting for permission."

"More than you do. What're you doing exactly?"

"What I feel like. What *you* feel like." She offered her little finger to the finch or whatever it was. "I love him. Dinky darling."

"Make me jealous," I said, "and I'll tell you to wring its neck if you're not careful."

"Tell me?" she said.

"And have you like it." I bent down to her. "Remember who you aren't."

We were walking past where two red-caps were flogging someone's recalcitrant slave; unless it was his pleasure, as it was certainly his right, to pay them to deal with the man for what he had yet to do. The owner was talking, seriously it seemed, with Marcus Furius, who had come to a recent reading of mine. Did his companion really say "hambush", meaning "ambush?" The slave's screams were pitched very loud, promise to his master that he was getting more than his money's worth. Reticence is a fool's conceit; some scream, others write verses.

"Mind your manners, sonny. Unless you want six yourself."

"You dare," she said, close against me.

Furius winked at me over the slave's owner's shoulder. I winced and ducked my head to one side. Furius said something to the man about the impression he was making, which disposed him, with a look at me, to halt the flogging, quite as if he had never commissioned him to be so vigorous.

"Who's the toady?"

"A certain Arrius," Clodia said, "*nouveau* not all that *riche*, one of Crassus's house dogs, kept on a golden lead, available to yap when required."

"Cheeky," I said.

"Home," she said, "before I'm missed."

Did he do nothing but scribble and serve his lady? He walked in her light, not always in her presence. He dined out; he gave readings; he amused the company with smartness that veiled his secret smart. A woman might have guessed his secret, certainly that he had one, or wished that he did; never another poet.

> *"Well, little sparrow, who's my darling's darling then?*
> *Does she like to play with it, gentle it at her breast?*
> *Does she, get it to stretch its little beak*
> *To tip her finger, provoke the little pecker's peck?*
> *My shining love, glittering passion,*
> *Does she have her little game? Does she,*
> *To ease her blues? I do believe so.*
> *When can I play with you as my darling does,*
> *And have you twitter my sorrows away?"*

I gave her time to purse her lips and smile, solemn eyes.

> *"I'll look as sharp as that sharp girl, they say,*
> *When a little golden apple rolled up and*
> *Undid her, undid her belt, her girdle,*
> *Tipped her into love's toll-free zone."*

"Deserting me, are you, because I love my little dicky-bird?"

"Of course. And because my brother Manlius is getting married."

"You love Sirmio more than you do me, sir *mio*. Hurry back or I shall have to seek consolation." Her finger-tip was titbit for the bird to pink.

"I'm caged as he can never be, wherever I go."

"Will you tell him about me, your brother?"

"I shall coin him a hymenaeal hymn and be back before you know it. So be careful! Meanwhile try this for size:

> "*Hadvantages, quotha (meaning advantages),*
> *Ditto hambush (for ambush), that's Arry:*
> *Boasting out loud how helegantly he spoke:*
> *Hambush hambitiously hemphasised;*
> *His mother's the same, and uncle Freedman,*
> *Mother's dad and wayward wife, the same.*
> *Official news: Arry's orf to govern Syria.*
> *Our ears relax. Them Greeks? Need not worry:*
> *Smooth breathings will amputate his aitches.*
> *Breaking news, 'orrible hintelligence to hand:*
> *IONIAN SEA GETS ROUGH TRITEMENT:*
> *Arry dubbed it High-own-Ian. What helse?*"

"I shall miss you," she said, laughing a tear.

"Or else," I said.

"Love me as I love you and we shall both be happy."

I took that for an envoi as I rode north. I read her parting words, as she must have wished, as threat and promise, and then re-read them as warning not to take our love as seriously as I did; or was it as she feared I did not? Or... Oh the possibilities when vice is versified! I wrote a wedding song for Manlius and knew, unless it was hoped, that what bound me to Clodia, her to me, was richer than innocent, more binding, in my view, than any public celebration could make it. Did I envy

Manlius for the comeliness of his wedding, the provincial festivity? Or did I imagine how much he could envy me for having a consul's wife, metropolitan goddess, as my love? Variants swarmed in my head, twigs for kindling.

Sirmio was a reminder of simplicities which seemed now to make Manlius younger than I. I deceived him, nicely and with pleasure, as I did my parents, with the joy I claimed to find in what was now more memory than sanctuary. I played at being unchanged well enough to be so in their eyes. When I asked whether Solonaki was coming to the wedding feast, Manlius winced. "Father gave him his freedom. He hasn't been the same since. As a slave, he thought that he could never go home; now he *knows* he cannot. He lacks the heart and the legs and fears what he might find left of his memories. So he walks alone, more aggrieved than liberated by father's generosity."

"*Ti na kanoume;*" I said. "Nothing to be done, hard task that."

"You've been in Rome," Manlius said. "How about a swim?"

We repeated what had once been spontaneous, shaking wet heads at each other and plunged for the shore, as if we were boys. I edited what I had written for the wedding and gave myself a happy part:

> "*Garland your hair with marjoram,*
> *Soft-scented; veil your face, come*
> *Smiling down to us, saffron shoes,*
> *Milk-white feet!*"

I took the solo role for myself and coached the chorus:

> "*Awake, awake this happy day*
> *Join in lusty marriage songs…*
> *Join the dancing, hold it high*
> *The marriage torch!*"

I came in again with:

"For Junia comes to Manlius,
As Venus of Idalium
Came to Paris...lovely girl,
Blessed by the gods...
Lovely as flower-heavy myrtle,
Toy of forest nymphs, each branch
Their darling, tipped with blossom,t
Pearled with dew."

I broke off and wrote, as if with another pen:

"What woman can claim that she was ever loved
(And tell the truth) as Lesbia by me?
What bond was ever struck as fast, as true,
As the love in me that's found in loving you?"

My secret wedding took first place with me. By not telling Manlius about my love, I kept Lesbia to myself and hoped, I suppose, that she would do the same. And then I was back with the chorus.

"Call the new mistress to her home,
Eager for her husband, twine her heart
Close with love, as ivy binds
Tight to the tree."

My cue for:

"With golden steps, lady beloved
Of the gods, step forward, cross
The polished threshold."

I thought of Lesbia and her promise, if promise it was, to come with me if I could find a safe house.

"No woman can say that she was loved
(And tell the truth) as Lesbia is by me.
No bond was ever struck as fast, as true,
As the love in me I found in loving you."

The chorus came in with *"O Hymen, Hymen, Hymenaeus O!"* My cue
for:

"Soon let a baby Manlius
Reach out soft hands from mother's breast,
Laugh at his father...
...baby lips parted in glee.
Let him grow so like his father
That all acknowledge him
Noble as Manlius, modest
As Manlius' wife."

I took time out to note in my secret pages:

"Your questions, Lesbia, are these:
How many kisses to sate, how many
To surfeit my passion? Go to Cyrene,
Count the grains of Libya's sands,
The whole lasarpiciferous desert..."

I could feel – or did I crave? – the sting of Solonaki's switch, see those
half-closed eyes, tilted head, and had to tell him, "It means bearing an
alliaceous fruit". The head went back, eyes slits; he sighed approval.

"...begin where Jupiter breathed hot tips
For his oracle's Ammonian branch,
And on to old Battus' holy sepulchre.
Number the numberless stars
That look down in the wordless night

On men that are out to steal kisses.
To kiss you as often as that
Would sate any normal madman,
And your Catullus perhaps,
Too many for the peepingest Tom
To count or get his tongue around!"

The chorus came in with:

"Girls, close the doors now. Our part
Is done; and you, the happy pair,
God bless you. Enjoy one another,
Undying gift of the gods.
O Hymen, Hymenaeus, O!"

We feasted, we drank, we sang. I sat with my love, her absence, and acted as if I were one with the company. I hoped Lesbia was no happier than I was; and then tortured myself, deliciously, imagining otherwise. As evening came on, my father accepted a thoughtful rug from my mother and wished he had not looked old enough to need it. He asked how things were in Rome; it might have been the moon, he had been there seldom and now relied on my eyes to see it at all.

"Apart from expensive? Merely momentous."

"And what are you contributing, in the momentous line?"

"I sing my songs for sixpences, more and more of them, the spicier I make them. I've been Solonakied by Marcus Tullius, no less. He thinks me a dissident Greekling because my verses fail to be as plonkety-plonk as his own, composed ad nauseam in his own well-deserved honour. He means well and does only almost as well. My friend of a kind, Publius Clodius is moving to have him exiled. Meanwhile, Tully's happy to show people, the best people or better, his new lemon-wood table which cost more, he's glad to announce, than a fleet of triremes."

"Where does the money come from?"

"Grateful clients, I suppose, and also – my friend Caelius suspects –

from those generous enough to hope to be spared the sharpness of his public perorations. A lawyer's most rewarding clients are ones he never goes to court for. Or *piuttosto* against."

"Julius was here again not long ago. He's still offering to take you with him to Gaul. Richer pickings, he says, than even he'd been told. Good experience, the military. A bit of northern air would do your lungs good. You could bring home a Druid to do your laundry."

"I'd sooner go east and nab myself a Dryad."

"You're quick to be quick, Gaius. Are you hiding something?"

"The emptiness of my purse, not very successfully."

"You need a rich wife."

"I'm wedded to Thalia, never Calliope."

"Solonaki told me, very early, that showing off was the great impediment to your progress. A poet can fall very heavily over his own feet."

"You never spoke to me before, father, in quite this…register. Am I perhaps more like you than I ever thought myself?"

"Business keeps a man prosaic. Age grows wisdom that he can fling like rice; and is as little picked up. That number you wrote for Manlius suggests a certain envy."

"Politeness always hides something."

"You're pleased to be gnomic." Father's sour flattery came from some source I had never guessed him to have. "How do you get your poetry known in the right places?"

"By delivering it in the stews," I said. "Nothing like promising to shock people to get them to come to low places. *Cave canam*, as the bitches say. Watch out or I may sing."

He had chosen to smile. "Do you also circulate copies?"

"Unless you knew I did, in whatever small numbers, you would scarcely know to ask, would you, father?"

"Are we ever to see some?"

"I doubt whether they would mean much to you."

"I shall take that to be complimentary."

"Roman gossip doesn't always travel well, especially when ripe."

He said, "I'll give you some more money when you leave. You need to entertain, I imagine, if you wish to be known as entertaining."

"Not my only ambition, father. But I should be grateful."

"Manlius is going to Rhodos and points east. I've some useful contacts in those parts. If you need a windfall, might you consider going in with him?"

I said, "There's talk of some of us going on Gaius Memmius's staff when he goes to govern Bithynia. Caesar's old stamping ground."

"Rumoured to be an honest man, Memmius. But you mustn't hold that against him."

"Having married Sulla's daughter, he can afford the luxury of rectitude."

"Rarely a profitable quality," my father said. "When the governor elects to be scrupulous, his staff come home with no heavier baggage than they left with."

"But he does fancy himself a patron of the muses. Lucretius Carus promises to have made him immortal."

"And who might master Carus be? One more Greek in drag?"

"A poet, native born, who proclaims the happy virtues of Epicurus."

"Any good?"

"Hexametrically magniloquent, and at length; very earnest, which makes for want of variety, never mind levity. The drummer's drawback."

"And what does he say of you?"

"Nothing unpleasant, I don't think; or someone would have hurried to tell me of it."

"And yet you seek those people's company. Better to be found with Julius; certainly more...practical."

"That ever fatter pig Mamurra for instance."

"Brilliant engineer. Julius says he doesn't know where he would be without him."

"This side of all the Rubicons he elects to cross. Every bridge the porker builds helps his master to a bloody fortune."

"Bithynia, if you elect to go there, I've got people you can go and see, with profit, in that part of the world. Have you considered marriage yourself?"

"I am already engaged," I said.

"Oh?" I relished the flicker of alarm on the mercantile face.

"To Thalia."

"Rarely a paying proposition."

Why was it a comfort that father was so uncomfortable with me? Had my absence in Rome displeased him? My presence widened the distance between us. Had my lack of career in the big city deprived him of something to boast about? Perhaps my mother feared that she might not see me again. Roman mothers, like Spartan, were supposed to be proof against sheltering attachment, but public proprieties are ever at war with private truth; why else are they promoted? Was I sad to leave Sirmio again? Yes. Did I delay my return to Rome? No. Regret was the spur, departure its conclusion. My father gave me enough money to imply how little pleasure it gave him that I showed no signs of making a career in circles to which he had given me the key. It also served to maintain Valerian *bella figura*. Confident that Manlius and his bride, and their prompt progeny, would cheer my parents' old age, I left Sirmio younger than I had arrived.

My father's frowning generosity threw in a couple of home-grown slaves, Ater and Zeno, the former fruit from Jugurtha's army defeated by Marius, the latter from that of Mithridates the Great, pacified by the greater Cornelius Sulla, to the last man. Zeno told me that the king had taken so many doses of prophylactic poison that he had to order a slave to butcher him before Sulla could have the pleasure. Even the Cornelian slaughterer never matched Mithridates' clarion cull of eighty thousand Romans, mostly civilian. The massacre to oust the colonial power determined it to confirm its presence.

I was now up to renting a small house at the smarter, still loud and smelly, edge of the Suburra. I gave dinner parties, counted spoons, flyted with the brightest.

> "Asinius, of the Marrucinian tribe!
> Yes, you: I spotted what your left hand was doing,
> While we're laughing and drinking,

You whip people's napkins for fun.
Smart work, do you think? I don't.
Cheap and nasty, odd way to make friends.
Exaggerate, do I? Ask brother Pollio.
He'd shell out for you to change your way.
Your bro is a chap with charm and wit,
Who doesn't stoop to stealing for laughs.
Stand by for three hundred lines
Of choice abuse, or give back my linen.
No matter what it might be worth.
They're presents from absent friends,
Saetaban napkins expressed
By Fabullus and Veranius,
Napery I'm bound to love as well
As little Veranius and my own Fabullus."

Pain and pleasure kept me from going immediately to her house. I longed to see her, touch her lips, smile at her quickened breath, if quicken it did, feather the breasts with my palms, implying more. At the same time, in the same spirit (here was oddness), I savoured what I hoped would be her puzzlement when she heard that I was back in Rome and had not hurried to see her, toyed with her fear that I was amusing myself elsewhere. I walked past her house several times, entertained myself with sauntering indifference. Had I not longed to see her, I should not have had that sweet sense of deceit. I acted as though she were watching me, guilt and innocence in one; life enriched by my performance of myself. When finally I chose to put an end to my delicious cruelty, to her, to me, I rehearsed breathlessness, fancied having her believe that I had come as soon as I could.

She did not move from her couch in the shaded room. "How did it go?"

I said, "You sound..."

"I am," she said.

"Unwell?"

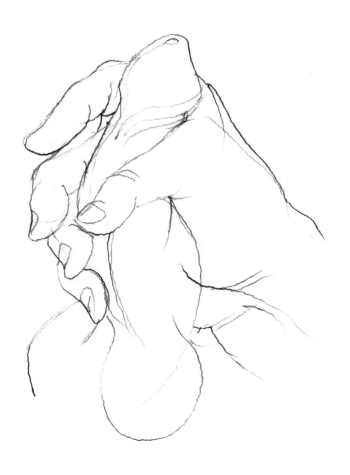

"Perhaps you don't know. Or care. He died."

"Celer? Did he? When was this?"

"I looked at his cage one morning and he was…he was lying in the bottom. Poor little thing. When I picked him up, he weighed no more than…one heavy feather."

"Nice figure!" I said. "Poor you."

"Don't touch me. I'm very…tender."

"I've got the very thing for it."

"This isn't the time."

"We'll get you another one, *vigil ales*."

"It won't be the same."

"Whom have you seen," I said, "while I was stuck in the sticks?"

"The Styx indeed," she said, "I'm in mourning. Some people respect that."

> *"Who can stand and look at it?*
> *Who can look and stand it?*
> *A rooting pig maybe,*
> *And a dicey one at that,*
> *Unspoiled Gaul despoiled,*
> *Distant Britain poached!*
> *Romulus, you're fucked, sad faggot;*
> *How do you like him, cock of the walk?*
> *All set are you, to call him Adonis?*
> *Camp as may be, can you truly fancy that?*
> *Rooting porker, I call him,*
> *And a dodgy one at that."*

I relished the disquieted murmur of the audience. Having gone too far, they dared me to go further. Where else?

> *You two supplied the softening sauce,*
> *Caesar and pom-te-pom Pompey,*
> *Mamurra the blot on your scutcheon*
> *While you pull the plug on the world."*

Did I expect a gasp at my insolence? They laughed; happy disappointment. Seeing my friend Flavius make a little face (poets often do when another hits the mark), I rewarded them with a change of diet:

> *"Flavius, this little dish of yours,*
> *No wit, no style, am I right? Wrong?*
> *Then why so reluctant to tell me?*
> *Some phithysicky crumpet, is she,*
> *So hot for it you can't get a word out?*
> *Don't tell me you're tossing alone at night.*
> *Your bedroom tells a loud story:*
> *Boudoir bouquets. Syrian perfume,*
> *Pillows, left and right, pummelled,*
> *Your rickety pallet a case of the shakes,*
> *From back and forthing on tottery pins.*
> *No good not spilling the obvious beans.*
> *Why? Fucked out messing about?*
> *So whatever she's like, angel or slag,*
> *Tip me the wink and your praises I'll sing,*
> *Or I might just send you up instead."*

Fabullus grinning, I pulled this one from my repertoire:

> *"You're going to eat like a king, Fabullus,*
> *Chez moi in a couple of days,*
> *Assuming the gods send you well,*
> *And provided you bring the supplies*
> *(Quality and quantity, please)*
> *First a suitable charmer,*
> *Wine and wit and a cache of giggles,*
> *Pick them up on the way, dear boy,*
> *And you'll not go short of a feast.*
> *Out of funds, me? My wallet's bulging…*
> *With cobwebs. Will you take a draught of love?*

No pro quo could be quidder than this,
Exclusive from Venus, Cupid and co.
One sniff of my mistress's secret scent
And you're down on your knees,
Praying the gods to make you all nose."

Manlius Torquatus came up to me as the audience dispersed, smiling, apart from the poets, Ravidus, Ravenna's raven their cackling convener. Manlius patted his hands together in discreet salute.

"Enjoyable stuff, Catullus! Who is she?"

I said. "My bed's as empty as my wallet. That bit was all too true."

"Your eyes tell a different story, not to mention your reputation."

"Trust one poet to rumble another."

"What about her bed, whoever she is?"

I said, "I never get nearer than near it."

"She has a husband."

"Is indeed the problem."

"She's never the first. May I show you some of my verses? You'll see I have some experience of...the clandestine. No small part of the pleasure, I find, deception."

"I used to think the same."

"What woman is wholly grateful for being trusted? It smacks of hinting that she has no choice."

"That poem was written before I even met her."

"First, I don't believe you, master C.; secondly you're as good as telling me she exists. Do I know her?"

"No one does," I said, "not as I do. Or could."

"A man of position, I take it, the *marito*."

"I am not your witness, Manlius Torquatus, and won't be drawn. Please respect that."

"I have my suspicions."

"How would you not? Rome is Rome."

"You think she can't...accommodate you. Or is that she won't?"

"We have nowhere to go and be...undisturbed."

My predicament amused him. "You lack a friend who won't tell while you kiss. Or where."

"Let me know," I said, "when you're next doing a reading and I'll bring my loud laugh to prompt the criticules."

"You're quicker to arms than a German to beer. I have a house out on the Appia I use only occasionally. You're welcome to take your eminent lady there. I'll tell my janitor to leave the keys in the pot by the door. No one will be any the wiser and you can pipe a happy paean or two, if she comes up to scratch. Make a change from all that bitchery, master C."

"You don't see what I write about her; and fail to put about."

"When it's all over you can pay me by telling who she is, was."

"It never will be," I said, "over. She's incurable."

I went home and scratched some lines for Fabullus's friend:

> "*Veranius, I'm not short of friends;*
> *I've three hundred thousand and counting,*
> *So happens you're number one.*
> *So you're chez vous again, re-united*
> *With your brothers and your aged mama?*
> *You're here, happiest news I could have.*
> *I'm longing to hear the lowdown,*
> *Who's who, what's what, and where*
> *in España. Can't wait to deliver an abrazo,*
> *Kisses on that grinning mouth, those eyes!*
> *I mean it, happy men, however many there be,*
> *Who could be happier than I am?*"

Courtesy put me in a good humour. It cued me to:

> "*Come, join the mourners, come gods of love,*
> *Gods of desire, whoever loves Venus first,*
> *Come join the dirge. Death has struck my love.*

Her sparrow's dead, my darling's darling,
Who cared for him more than her very eyes,
Dead, who knew his mistress better than a girl
Her mother. He was never out of her lap,
Jumping here, jumping there, jumping back.
As soon as he saw her, up he piped and piped
For no one else. Now it's over forever.
Down that dark tunnel he's gone, whence, they say,
Once vanished, you never rise again.
To hell with you, you shades of Hell,
You get us all down in the end,
Even the most beautiful. Her beautiful sparrow
You won't even spare us. It's cruel.
It's murder! Poor little bird!
In passing, sparrow, do you know
That you went and made Lesbia weep?
Her eyes are red-rimmed and puffy,
You've actually made them look small."

Good humour primed happy malice:

"What loony idea, cher Ravidus,
Makes you lock horns with Catullus?
Whose name have you taken in vain
That he's driven you raving bonkers?
Or is it all public relations?
Making a name for yourself, sonny?
You will. Unless you lay off my love,
I'll scribble my name on your spine
And you can quote me."

The rumour was that Ravidus was jealous not of my verses but of my affection for Juventius, his for me. It was my petty pleasure to stick it to him. I was still smiling when I heard a tap on the open door behind me.

"Gaius, may I?"

I recognised the voice without looking round and said, "Just the man, Salaput! I'm stuck for an anapaest, if you have a ripe one with you." He said nothing, stood by my shoulder. I looked up.

"My dear friend, what's happened?"

"Quintilia. And the baby."

I stood, then crouched to embrace him; my tears, his eyes on the tablet where I had been scratching my verses. "Time you did something... major," he said. "Before it's too late."

I opened my mouth; and shut it again. I waited for him to say something. He seemed so charged with anguish that he could produce only its sad sedative, resignation. I cleared my face of the vain humour I had been wearing.

"You're the only person I've told."

I bent and kissed his forehead. What is not made public can seem never to have happened. I told myself to remember that. Pain becomes reproach, unsolicited blight on good humour, scars our luck, loses friends.

> "*No answers meet us from the grave, dear Calvus,*
> *Yet might our pain still touch them there?*
> *The grief lost love brings to life again?*
> *Death that came too soon hurts Quintilia*
> *Less, for knowing that you love her still, so much.*"

"Very touching," my darling said. "How long did it take you to write?"

"I was in a hurry to see you. I'll polish it later. I've found a place."

"Have you? To do what?"

"To do when. Our chance comes. Outside the *porta* Capena. Villa with a walled garden. Disused *maison secondaire*. No one will ever see you, except me. Belongs to a good friend of mine, not close, but...reliable."

"*Porta* Capena! Very...appropriate! When you've had your triumph, you can stop to leave a tribute in the Temple of Mars and then come back through it. Better yet, borrow an elephant or two from Gnaeus P. and ride in."

"Tight fit."

"Have you told this friend of yours that it's me you want to… entertain?"

"I've told him only that it's the most beautiful woman in Rome."

"Then you have," she said. "Are you paying him?"

"He's a fellow poet, of the rare breed that doesn't need the money. He wrote the naughty one about Lucretia killing herself not because she'd been raped, but because she enjoyed Sextus Tarquinius more than she ever had her husband. The sweet surprise of enforced pain."

"And now you want to play Sextus."

I said, "I love you more at this moment—"

"Than ever you will afterwards."

"— than you can possibly imagine."

"I leave imagining to you. It's your forte. Perhaps I should refuse. You write better when you're denied."

"You're not afraid of…*him*, are you?"

"Your pen frightens me more, and what you might do with it, if…disappointed."

"Would you be pleased, truly, if I promised never to write another word about you? I'll tell the world that it's always been Juventius really, my truest love. And it'll be true. If you'll be him again."

"Can I trust you?"

"To love you forever? I fear I shall whether you trust me or not."

"More threat than promise, that. Love includes betray and almost craves it. How do we get there? How do I in particular? Your friend's place."

"Remember the slave girl I took to the market? Invisible, wasn't she?"

"We shall have to wait till Celer is out of the city."

"I love you more at this moment…"

"Than you ever will again?"

"…than you can well imagine."

"I leave imagining to you," she said. "It's what you do best."

"You have yet to know what I do best."

"One minute you love me forever, the next you'll be sizzling me on a rack of words, titbits for snacking snickerers and calling it immortality."

"I will never write a cruel word about you."

"Unless what?"

"You deserve it," I said.

"What's his name, this friend?"

"He doesn't know yours. Best not know his. Call him Allius; A.N. Other. You're not still upset, are you?"

"About...?"

"Your little feathered friend."

"Bloody bird!" she said.

I kissed and kissed her until her lips were bleeding; mine too, her neat teeth.

Caelius came up beside me in the forum, threaded his arm under mine, walked on as though he carried some dangerous secret. "Caesar got word of your latest Mamurra number."

"Has he taken offence?"

"I rather think he has. He wants you to come to dinner."

Julius greeted me at his door. "Poor Marcus Tullius – you've heard how they ransacked his house on the Janiculum when he went into exile? Dangerous to accumulate enviable possessions and lack the force to protect them. When an outsider hopes that the quality will be grateful for the service he renders them, he dreams of turning clouds into stepping stones."

"I'm never likely to be in that condition."

"I hope you didn't expect a large company."

"I expected nothing, unless your displeasure."

"On what count? Oh, your verses? I laughed; was I not supposed to?"

"I'd sooner you told me how vexed you were."

"My dear fellow, you should hear what the men say about me when

92

I walk around the camp in a quiet cloak. You have a very civilian view of life. You and Tully both imagine the world can be shamed into being virtuous: he with a gravy of superlatives and a retinue of worthy references, you with the pepper and salt of your Attic models."

"None of them Athenian."

"No? Aeschylus could be tart enough when he took a holiday from polysyllables: 'Trust me to spot a hot young piece with a taste for cock...'"

When he paused, I completed the couplet: "'I'm quite the connoisseur when it comes to fillies like that'. Actaeon, wasn't it?"

"You took the bait," Caesar said. "quite as I guessed. A trick learned from the great Hannibal: offer what seems an irresistible opening and trust a proud man to accelerate triumphantly into the trap."

"And what kind of mouse does that make me?"

Caesar said: "This is not a city in which it pays to be nothing but caustic."

"I have no mind to be paid."

"Nor yet the means to dispense with patronage, if only your father's. Which is, in part, why I asked you to share this informal snack. I'm careful with my diet."

"Having a long way yet to march."

"And back. Can be the longer road. Rest immured in Rome, you may never move again; no place for ducks to sit in with impunity."

"I don't see myself in the quack's role," I said.

"Insolence is deference in drag; no substitute for a career. The young poet is full of promise, the old spent squibs."

"That depends on the work he's done."

"And also, my dear Catullus, on living long enough to do it. That cough of yours might profit from an absence from the city. Go somewhere less...insalubrious and who knows what more...sustained work you might produce."

"Unless my muse is here."

Julius looked at me. "Allow yourself to be dependent on a woman's favour and you've made Circe your master."

"Unless she's Calypso."

"Even the delicious Calypso inclined Odysseus to carpentry, did she not? I wish you joy of whatever it pleases, or pains, you to do. No necessary distinction there. Having no envy, I have small interest, although I probably know, as the world does, more than a clever young man supposes. You have a talent for making enemies. Do you have the muscle to floor them?"

I said, "I write verses. A citizen is still at liberty in that regard at least."

"Might that not show how little importance power attaches to the arts?"

"As artists to power."

"Greeks can be Greek, wherever they live. The Parthenon made claim to centrality, but *hoi men Athenaioi* were too conceited, and too tight, to lavish citizenship on others. We've learnt from their mistakes, slowly and painfully; other people's folly teaches us more than their good example. What matters in Rome is your clout not your wit."

I said, "You deplore the moralists, then moralise."

He measured me another *copita* of Signine, deserved medicine. "Let me infuriate you further. You will prove yourself appetising, if never indispensable, to the lady more by your absence than by...assiduous attendance. Come with me to Britain. Fat pickings still dangling to be plucked. Return rich; and when you do, you'll find ambitions quite other than bedroom mountaineering."

"If I come back at all. Your mechanical friend would probably take the chance to topple me from one of those bridges of his."

"You accuse him of vulgarity, the invaluable Mamurra. He is indeed vulgar, but no more so than your friend – oh and mine, and mine! – Publius C. It depends only on the register. No wise man goes on campaign with a mere entertainer. Alexander soon shed his eulogist when he turned troublemaker."

"So much for callisthenics," I said.

"Who takes a reference is also liable to take the bait and dullards will reel him in. Mamurra's a pontifex to merit the title."

94

I said, "Memmius has been given Bithynia to govern next year. He's already asked Gaius Helvius to be of his company."

"Cinna? None better," Caesar said, "except in a tight corner."

"Not a notable Bithynian resource. They want me to bring the salt."

"I'll put it plainly, young Catullus. Come and be a man or resign yourself to being a connoisseur of disappointments. Never imagine you can't go on campaign and still have time for writing. Quintus Cicero, with me in Gaul, wrote four tragedies in sixteen days; even his brother gave him best; if not better. Your father, equitable as he is, would be pleased to know you on a horse."

"Father has my energetic brother Manlius to honour his hopes. I prefer Epicurean modesty."

"So you boast. Did you suppose that I asked you here to warn you that Mamurra might rent a blade to prune your foliage? I doubt that he's even aware of your barbs. Oh I know, I know, they're not aimed at him. More at your father perhaps."

"I noticed how you looked at my mother."

"Are you ashamed of yourself for thinking such a thing?"

"I didn't think it; I said it. You know what I meant."

"Whatever you do, or don't, get away from proving to Roman society how little you care for its favours; it smacks of soliciting. Meanwhile, would you care to render me a small service?"

"Anything short of *proskynesis*. I'm with Callisthenes in that department."

"Cast a critical eye on some verses of mine."

I have to say I respected his even look. I smiled first. He touched my shoulder.

I told Caelius about it at the pot-house our "family" favoured, where reputations were always on the griddle. "I shall advise him to hit the Belgians with his elegiacs when the wind's in their direction. They'll drop their shields to hold their noses."

Caelius said, "Are they as bad as all that?"

"I have yet to read a line," I said. "The great Solon's verses weren't up to much either."

"Memorable though. He took some trouble to find a way of being in your debt, Julius. Generosity of a kind. Why do you suppose?"

"Not for fear of my Archilochan shafts. I'm *sans* illusions in that department. Funny how often generals have read rather more than one supposes."

During those days, however many, while waiting for Celer to do something consular to draw him outside the city, did Catullus do nothing but dwell on pleasures to come? Or did her promise release him from daily attendance? He was never happier than at the prospect of happiness, unless it was when making people laugh:

> "PRETTY BOY SEEN WITH AUCTIONEER.
> *Rumour has it: going, going, gone."*

He dined out; he gave dinner parties; he enjoyed what he had yet to enjoy. The day dawned when Celer and his designated legion went to remind some festive Italian city that Rome was Rome.

> *"She never came, bride on her father's arm*
> *To that dark house, rich with Assyrian balm;*
> *Secretly she crept, that miracle night, to me;*
> *Peerless present, filched from marito's lap,*
> *Yes, it's enough, yes, if that one time will cap*
> *Her calendar of love, and prove its apogee.*
> *Allius, our salvation, slid us the keys:*
> *a secret drive, covert space to love*
> *And love ad lib., my mistress and I,*
> *Then in she steps, my white goddess,*
> *Creak of sandal on dipped threshold..."*

More slur than creak? She stood there against the door-framed moon, boyish as a Spartan bride, until she shed cloak, loosened hair. As she closed the door, nervous lamplight made me tremble. She unsleeved herself from her slave clothes, without haste, eyes on me as mine on her. "He has never seen me like this," she said.

The first time was only the first time; the second good enough for her to say that she was sated. The next time, never the last, I felt a surge of rage, that she should so soon have had enough, or say she had. I took her in the Alexandrian style, as if she had refused me. I turned her and took her "no" for "yes". She gasped, cried out and worked her urgency against mine. When she caught her breath, she smiled as she never had before. "Sextus Tarquinius, are we? Beast."

I walked home with a different step, possessor possessed.

> "God bless you, Allius, you and your truest love!
> Be happy in the house you made ours that time…
> Kind friend, who kindled all my happiness.
> Dearer to me, my mistress, now, than I to myself!
> My luck, she's but to live and I am more alive!"

"The telling is more delicious than any…kissing, am I right? Say I'm not and I shall know I am."

"You're not," I said. "And I'm no Cretan."

"Every lie plays porter to secret truths, is that your point?"

"She's the only woman I shall ever love. I'm only worried that while I'm in Asia…"

"Don't worry; because she almost certainly will. Put her out of your mind. Expect nothing, you'll not be disappointed; unless disappointment is your fancy."

"You don't know her, Rufus. What she is now. What we are, to each other. I'm only afraid she'll be unhappy without me."

"Enjoy Bithynia is my advice, up to the hilt. You'll then come home exactly as she would wish, with no interest in what she did or – less likely – didn't do in your absence, and small wish to tell her what you did if you did as you should."

"You're my best friend, I want you to –"

"Best and busiest, Gaius V. I've got these Egyptians who want me to swing things for them in high places, by whatever low means."

"– watch out for her. She's very vulnerable. She's going be lonely. She said as much."

"Never take such threats too seriously. Clodia lonely?"

"She means it."

"And if you mean to keep her, tell her to do as she pleases and ask no questions when you get back."

"I shall be easier in my mind, if I know you're keeping an eye on her."

"Depend upon it," he said. "My prescription for you to have an easy mind is three hotsies a night, if you insist on not overdoing it. No trouble in Bithynia and not much else to do, especially if you elect to go there under the aegis of an honest man. Persuade the good Memmius to commission you to whack out an epic or two."

"I think of her as my wife, Caelius."

"Evidence that she isn't."

'Her fan-carrier to Clodia Metelli. Greetings from the flaming ramparts, eastern section. Just as I feared, but hotter, Bithynia is Hades with no sign of Helen, Phaedra or Dido. My friend Gaius Helvius Cinna has done just a little to alleviate the loneliness I feel without you. He went straight to work on a mini-epic, title *Zmyrna*, and promises that if I do the same I shall find the time passes more quickly before we are back in Rome, so I am setting out to match him with a little number on the Argonauts, nothing like the long and winding Rhodian's version, but stitched cleverly enough to make Marcus Tullius gnash those antique tusks.

'It seems likely that I shall come home with a trunk full of hexameters and not much else. Memmius is proving as honest as he threatened to be: he won't have any of us screw a useful penny out of the natives. Just my luck! When we all get home, with empty pockets, I shall probably press Rufus to sue the old boy for malpractice. Don't say honest governors never get what's coming to them. Now tell me about the upper rogues' gallery, who's doing what and to whom? Tell me that you miss me, I shall wonder what you are doing to alleviate the pain; tell me that you're not, the pain will mine.'

"Did you get letters, Gaius Helvius?"

"One or two."

"What's going on? What are you afraid to tell me? Tell me!"

"Metellus Celer is dead. Your Clodia is…a free woman. Why do you look like that?"

"Dead how?"

"Tully would have it that madame did him in."

"Never. Why would she?"

"Are you just slightly afraid lest she means to hold you to something you never expected to be called upon to honour?"

"I don't know what I am," I said.

"Precisely so," Helvius said.

I did not smile back. "I shall have a better idea as soon as I get back to Rome."

"Does that dispose you to hurry? What are you waiting for?"

Caelius Rufus took chance for his leader. Quick to enjoy whatever opportunities the dice might roll his way, he had something in common with the wide spill of post-Alexandrine Greeks. Once the justice of Zeus no longer promised them his favour nor any regular sense of the world, they made Tyche, *Lady Luck, their principal deity. Caelius honoured Roman civility as the new poets did imported prosody, with sly homage. His wit was the measure of his pride. Ambition without scruple, desire without design, charm without promise, such were the ingredients of his impersonation of the best of company. He called on Clodia Metelli as the tenets of civility allowed and as soon as impudence could lend them piquancy.*

"Why the long face, Clodia Metelli? Right and proper wear in public, but no need to parade it when you're alone with me. In private, you can bask in your freedom. Anything I can do, as they say…"

"I should be nothing but a trophy to you," she said. "Deny it."

"And have you lose interest? If I please you, you can enjoy it; if not, nothing is lost, for either of us. Come what may, or may not, you have your freedom. I have no wish to deprive you of it."

"Am I to like you because you're shameless?"

"I can promise only what no honest simpleton has the wit to offer: I shall never curse you with my trust and the sour suite of expectations that goes with it."

"And you call Gaius Valerius your friend! You're the one man he relies on to keep wolves from my door. What kind of a fox does that make you?"

"An honest one. I shall cede place to him, gladly, when he gets home. If he's wise enough to ask no questions, he'll receive no unwanted answers."

"Unless I let him have them."

"I trust you're too clever to do that. And love him too much. If you do."

"You'd have me be the bitch of bitches so that you can treat me badly and claim I deserve it. There's only one reason why I'm tempted, no more than tempted..."

"And no less, is that?"

"...to be amused, let's say, by your treachery."

"On the contrary. He said he relied on me to take care of you."

"And how contrary is that? You're more cynical than the meanest dog that hustles for scraps at Crassus' back door."

"Why do you suppose Gaius went to Bithynia?"

"I don't suppose; I know: he went because he had no choice. His Sabine father threatened to tighten the strings on his money-bag."

"Is what he chose to tell you. 'Who weeps with one eye winks with the other', isn't that what Publilius says?"

"You know these provincial *equites*. Money's all they can imagine anyone caring about."

"Of course I know. Why else do shenatorials rely on them to do their business?"

"It's better you not come to this house any more."

"As you wish. Where do you propose we go?"

"If I have anything more to do with you, Caelius Rufus, I know exactly what will follow. Meaningless....*futationes*."

"Then how can you hesitate, Clodia Metelli?"

"Does it not occur to you that I love him?"

"I'm depending on it," he said. "Shall we play at being serious? If you love him as much as I don't doubt you do, you'll know that the greatest service you can render him will be to give him good reason to find himself the rich wife that famously empty purse of his needs, without the curse of a conscience or a backward glance."

"If that was what he wanted..."

"It's what every Roman of quality needs; what he wants comes later. The man who has to sing for his supper rarely eats as well as he'd like."

"You don't know him as I do. No one does."

"You've made him into what you want him to be. Why do you suppose that he found you irresistible? Because he was an innocent provincial who had no idea of your reputation? Because he wanted to test himself on Rome's great challenge. He got in deeper than he ever intended. Men do, my beauty, with you."

"He made me feel something no else ever had."

"It's pretty to say so; but who brought him to your house and what had he not failed to warn him about you?"

"Are you trying to make me hate you, Caelius R.? You're certainly succeeding."

"What better approach to the most fascinating woman anyone ever met?"

"And you want to make Circe of me, if not Medusa."

"Hard as it may be, stone is not what you're turning me into."

"You'd like to think he's ruining himself for the sake of someone not worth having."

"And who is that?"

"If she believes a word you say, you'll think her the bitch of bitches. Which will suit you very well, as your reputation promises."

"There you are," he said.

"That smile…"

"Matches what you're thinking. Celer's death is enough to keep Gaius in Bithynia forever, unless…"

"I let him hear that I'm behaving?"

"Only if it suits you. It would certainly suit him."

"Betray him for his own good, is that what you recommend?"

"Would you have him a puppy forever? Why did he go to Bithynia in the first place?"

"We did that."

"Some of it," Caelius said. "It hurt him to tear himself away, but it also…"

"You think he set out to conquer me in order that I might hurt him? It suits you to think so; or have me believe it."

"Would he be the first hunter snagged in his own snare? You win men so easily you've never discovered what tricksters they can often be."

"He needed to play no tricks to have me…discover him to be something you could never be."

"He did what the young poet does best: sincerity his winning trick. By the time he had played it, he was his own victim."

"You think me not worth loving?"

"I think you irresistible; why else am I here?"

"Do you imagine that you're the first false best friend a man ever had?"

"I don't doubt that you've known dozens, dear Clodia. There's something particularly delicious in proving to yourself that no one is proof against your beauty, even if you despise a man for showing it."

"Gaius found something in me which others never suspected."

"Might that be because he put it there?"

"Sorry to disappoint you. You're right. It's what makes him unique."

"That it makes you so renders him precious to you. Before Gaius, you were one more Roman wife; he turned you into Erato."

"I don't rate that final 'o'; it sounds unfeminine."

"And I hate to see a beautiful woman deprived of pleasure."

"I shall be nothing to you but one more trophy. Do you deny it?"

"I promise."

> "*Swift craft bears him, Attis, over deep waters.*
> *Eager feet seek set out for the Phrygian grove,*
> *Thread hooped trees to the goddess's retreat,*
> *Mind awry, frenzy-frazzled, wits gone,*
> *Sharp flint...balls hanging heavy; and cut!*
> *Blood spurting, man unmanned, trailing blood,*
> *Eager white hands snatch up the tympany,*
> *Cybele's beat, great mother of mysteries,*
> *Soft fingers drum on tender hide, all girlish now,*
> *Shrill voice chants to her acolytes, dance,*
> *Dance to Cybele's covert! This way, this way,*
> *Lost flock rally to our lady of Dindymus!*
> *You came like exiles to an alien land,*
> *Braved salt currents, the sea's surly surge,*
> *Severed yourselves from Venus's lusty claims,*
> *Now dance, dance, dance for your mistress!*
> *No lagging, follow me, race, race to Cybele's*
> *Leafy lair. Cymbals clash, drums pound,*
> *Arched horns blow slow deep melodies,*
> *Rattle of kettledrums, Maenads toss*
> *Ivied hair, shrill voices hymn sacred virginity.*
> *Come where the goddess's chorus rock and roll,*
> *Restless feet, follow, dance faster, faster...*
> *So Attis, unman warbling unsongs*
> *To startling, mindless Maenad shrieks,*
> *Following drums, tambourines' clash,*
> *Leads the reckless rout to Ida's verdant slopes.*
> *Panting, frenzied, gasping for breath, lurching*
> *To his own beat through darkling woods,*

Attis the leader, wild heifer bucking
Against the yoke, eunuch priests in his wake,
Race to touch Cybele's sanctuary, collapse
Done-for dolls, spent, starvelings swoon.

In gentle quiet, furious frenzy seeped away.
But then the sun began to show his golden face,
Swept airy heaven, solid land, fluctuating sea
With flashing vigilance. His chargers put to flight
With sonorous hooves the nervous shadows of night.
Sleep, in alarm, quit Attis, took panic refuge
In divine Pasithea's tremulous breasts.
At that did Attis clear-eyed, look down and see,
Conscious what his own hands had wrought,
The sorry she that he now was, and would forever be.
With fevered heart, he forced himself to go
Back to the shore and gazed across the boundless sea,
Brimming with tears, remembered home and, all tears,
In wretchedness cried out his misery:

Oh land that sowed me, home that bore me,
And I deserted, as runaway slaves their master,
Stole to Ida's forests, where beasts huddle in frosted hides.
Now you are lost, my native soil, what refuge can I find?
Craving eyes turn despite myself towards you,
Brief reprieve from savage delirium.
Why, why, did I desert you for this emptiness?
Homeland, comfort, friends and parents,
Forum, school, the races, gymnasium.
Break my heart, break for miseries to come.
They loved me once, whatever form I took,
Female, young man, beardless youth, soft boy,
Flower of the gym, slick envy of the changing room,
Doorsteps crowded, all thresholds warm at sun's

Awakening and I rose up, my house aflower
With posies, garlanded and intricate.
And now must I be serving girl to the god,
Cybele's ingle, Maenad, half a self, human mule.
Sentenced to fir-clad Ida's shivering glaciers,
Life among Phrygia's towering peaks,
With scavenging deer and rooting boar.
What hurts I did to my wretched self were done.
Rosy lips let fly a woeful, carrying cry.
Cybele heard and was cued to ease the yoke
That harnessed her lions, urged the left one,
Scourge of livestock, 'Go, go, unleash your fury,
Have your lash madden him back to my precinct.
The fool who longed to flee my imperium.
Go flog your back with your own tail in rage
And utter roars that echo through the land,
Rumple tawny mane on bully neck.'
Then furious Cybele untied the reins, the beast
Lashed himself to rabid animosity,
Snarling, as though the thick brush he bounds.
Reaches the foam-fringed shore, and there
Saw the gentle Attis, girlified, by the marbled sea.
He roars and charges. The panicked victim flees
To the wildwood, lifelong maiden acolyte.

O goddess, great one, Cybele, god queen of Dindymus,
Pray visit none of your frenzies, madame, on my house.
Drive others crazy, others to frothing folly."

"What brought that one on, Gaius Valerius, pray?"

"Must be your proximity, Gaius Helvius, not to mention your facility. Every time I turn round you've added a hundred lines to *Zmyrna*. If they were as crappy as Suffenus, I could look you in the eye and congratulate you without hesitation, but damn you, G.H., they're going to last while the rest of us are blown chaff."

"You're probably right." He smiled like a friend. "Piss off. Time you did the big one, Gaius Valerius, and trumped us all. I fear you have it in you, not that I want you to know."

'Dear Gaius Valerius, I expect you've heard more news from Rome than you care to receive. I never imagined that I should find myself in the same sorry situation that I feared might be yours, in love. When Ourania left my house, I tried to shrug, as I have so often, and quickly smiled and dreamed of fresh cunt, fresh courage. How was Ourania different? I cannot say; that is the difference! How could she do what she did? Did I deserve it? Egnatius, I ask you, of all the toothsome men in the city. How clever you were to do as you did and be the first to leave! The gods rejoice in cruel twists; a man's friends are seldom slow to mimic them. I've always imagined that I was immune to the anguish soft lovers sing and blub about. My recipe was simple, worked very well until, suddenly (how else?), it ceased to work at all. Like you, I thought to make the muse my guide, by dancing to her skittish tune, Erato's I mean. I presumed I should taste all pleasure's recipes, sweet or sour, and move on each time to something fresh.

'When I had word of what was happening *chez* Clodia Metelli in your absence, and with whom, I guessed that you must have reckoned that the lady never offered love that lasted and timed things perfectly by choosing to run before you were cut. Did you fear that she might pay you out by remaining tearfully alone? As others must already have advised you, you were right not to fear such grasping fidelity *de sa part*. As always happens with lovers, we see the follies of others, and sometimes their astuteness, and hope that we can be among the wise when what so often happens to others happens to us. Why write all those glib verses celebrating the joys of deception and advocating compassionate heartless when it comes to saying goodbye, as if one was sorry to be going, unless it was because I saw, and feared, what might be coming?

'You have proved cleverer than I and, against what I expected, unless

I suspected it all along, more – what? – calculating. I wondered, after what you told me when you had spent that night in my house with madam, whether you were not as good as saying that you had had the best of all marriages – a single night of all you hoped for, never to be followed by whatever you might have dreaded. You cut yourself free as if – I know, because I heard it from her own lips – you truly regretted the escape which you declared your father had forced upon you. I smiled then and listened to her make excuses you were generous enough to garnish with tears. You will, I hope, be pleased to know that she loved you truly enough to be grateful for your promise that your love would never die. She sensed, as the sex does, the thorn within the garland – guessed that when you begged her to remain faithful in your absence, you were also telling her that she should not hope for reciprocity in that department. She knew men better than to hope for anything so improbable, if not unmanly; at the same time she appreciated your diplomacy. Exactly as you must have imagined, she has consoled herself for your absence by filling the vacant place in her bed.

'I am sentimental enough to assume that you indicated to Caelius that he should do what he could to assuage her regrets. She confessed, when I called on her, that she needed to summon all her courage to do as she did not doubt you planned: make your friend her consolation. She could see, she told me, without my asking, that you were ruining yourself for her sake and, because she loved you, she had to agree to seem cruel. Because she loved you, she had to hurt you, and leave you free as you did, she said, that little slave boy with whom you went to buy her the bird you dirged so callously about. She told me, because she thought it might suit my iambic skittishness, that women alone know the sweet sting that comes of renouncing what they least want to lose.

' "A woman of a certain age," she began to say, and then said, "all women are women of a certain age. They look back even when young and back again when older, forward always with dread." She said, and I suppose she meant it, that she was afraid that, if you ever came back, and she saw the tears you were certain to have the wit to shed, she would not be able to resist you. Think of me and smile, my dear Gaius, with a trace of pity, at the one who supposed himself immune to what you were so clever in avoiding. Be glad to know that madam C. has taken it very well and looks, to the casual eye, as beautiful and ageless as ever. I hope Memmius is making your journey worth the while and that when you return to us, you will put yourself in Julius's camp and make the political career which will lend your verses a passport to fame. I need hardly say how sorry I was to hear of the death of my namesake Manlius, your brother. In my present woeful state I could wish that he had lent me his fate.'

"*Your tearful letter, Manlius, I have it here.*
Crushed by misfortune, you say, and done for...
A ship-wrecked sailor on a foam-sudded beach...
Step poised, for solace, on the threshold of death...
Drag you back, should I, offer your heart
Some ease? 'Blessed Venus torments me...I toss, I turn,
Sorry singleton... The old sweet songs no consolation,
the Muses' lullaby...' Sleepless, you crave
A fresher tune, for friendship's sake, and love.

Dear Manlius, don't rate me unsympathetic,
I share your feelings, know the duty
Friend owes to friend. But, yes, I – like you -
Am fortune's toy, 'heart reft with pain'.
I passed the flowering springtime of my youth
In study rapt, began the day I came of age.
My special subject? Love, every gambit
That smiling goddess plays, her blend of joy and woe.
I was a star student, rated promising,
Until he died, my dear brother, filched from me,
Quenched my light. My happiness – alive
While you too lived – perished with your death.
You gone, I dropped my courses, interest gone
In all of pleasure's recipes. Hence, when you say,

'Things bad where you are, Catullus?
Here in Rome, the cream warms up
In a widow's bed…' I have to say I pass.
Pray understand, grief leaves no gifts
To offer. Here where I am, I've no table
Ripe with manuscreeds. My energy,
My youth, I left behind in Rome,
That's where I had my day, my floruit.
Here all I have is but a single bag.
No hard feelings, truly, but I can do
No more; affection, yes, I send, and gladly,
But the balm you seek, I'm fresh out just now.

This I must record, my dear divinities,
Manlius's kindness, his generous help.
Take up the story, muses, before these pages rust,
Save his name from time's oblivion,
'ere spiders lace obscuring shrouds
Round Manlius's invaluable renown.

When fickle Venus held my heart in thrall
Scorched was I by passion, and convulsed
With volcanic tides of love, eyes blinded,
Cheeks dewed with tears, as some rivulet
On a towering mountain-side
Goes bubbling down from rock to mossy rock,
Stream that once tumbled to the valley floor
Flows serene past stately poplar trees,
Refreshes the traveller on his sweaty way
And slakes parched pastures' thirsty furrows.
Such was my state – as when sailors lost at sea
In crow-black storms cry out in frantic need
To Castor and Pollux for a kinder breeze –
When Manlius proved my rescuer,

Granted us a private place, my love and me,
A secret bower where we might safely love.
Then in she glided, goddess mine, step sure
As a virgin bride's. Worn doorstep, moonlight feet.
Her sandal squeaked, remember? Happy moment.

So did Laodamia, first set foot
In doomed Protesilaus' place, hot with love,
Union unsanctified by sacrificed,
The gods above not pacified with blood.
O lady Nemesis, pray I never act
With that impertinent urgency.
Too late she learned, Laodamia,
A thirsty altar must be slaked with due blood
Before bride to insurgent groom submits.
He went; she waited. Winter came and went,
And came again, riling her starving heart
With love unsatisfied, schooling her to live
Without her man, snatched (the fates well knew)
For good, the day he went to fight at Troy."

I trekked to the Troad from Bithynia to mourn at the stump of the
Scaean Gate. No taller now than graves, the toppled towers, browsed
bald by tinkling goats, lame keeper huddled in saffron sheepskin. Verses
like ghosts auditioned in my brain, denying denial.

"Allius, Helen's rape the Argive princes called
To arms, to Troy summoned men to be men,
Troy, the damned, Asia's mass grave, Europe's too,
Heroes and their pride ground to common ash,
Now you've stolen my unhappy brother too,
Taken all light from life, our house our tomb.
Life's pleasures, every one, died with you, dear bro;
You gave my love its sweetest savour.

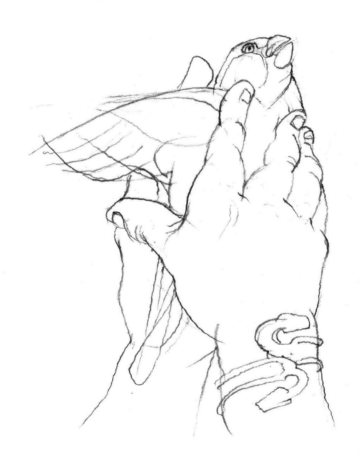

You lie, far from home, in no familiar company,
Ashes unaccompanied by kindred souls.
Bloody Troy, Troy joyless dumping ground
Clawed you down to lie in foreign soil.
They flocked back then, the flower of Greece,
Left their safe hearths, to troop to Troy
To halt the pleasure Paris took in a stolen whore
All couched in sumptuous laziness.
For this – for this! – fairest Laodamia,
Your husband, dearer than life's breath,
Was filched away; your love and his,
In passion's fever plunged to the abyss,
Fathomless as once was dug by Hercules,
So Greeks insist, at Pheneus, Mount Cyllene's base,
To drain the swamp and dry the fertile soil.
The so-called son of Amphitryon
Drilled through the mountain's very marrow,
Then the Stymphalian birds he nailed
At his mean master's ordinance.
Result: at heaven's gate new gods
Pressed in, and Hebe spared prolonged virginity.
Deep was that pit, but deeper yet your love
Was plunged when grief did down your pride.
Dearer he was to you than an only daughter's son
Born in time to warm a patriarch's waning heart,
His name inscribed as heir to all his riches
Puts paid to distant cousin's shameless scrounge
Playing vulture round that white-capped crown.
Did any dove ever so delight in her snowy
Other? That shameless harvester, they say,
Crops kisses with insatiable pecks, in love
More durable than ever heated woman's heart,
Save yours, Laodamia, you outdid their passion
Nestling, back then, with your brief golden boy.

Little or nothing did my beaming love yield to her
When she consigned herself to my embrace,
While all around her circled fluttered busy Cupid,
Gleaming all fresh in festive saffron rig.
And now, I'm told, a mere Catullus is not enough;
Better get used to madam's furtive flirts,
Not play the fool with unappealing pout.
Remember Juno, heaven's first lady,
Kept all her fury to herself when she well knew
How many, many peccadillos Jove was up to.
Not advisable, mortals, to compete with gods,
Nor rate my own 'gainst Juno's innumerable woes.
Did any voice call down from heaven to me
'Take on a husband's duties, relieve a shaking father
Of his burden'? Never did she come on father's arm
To that Assyrian-scented house,
No, secretly she did abscond, one marvellous night,
A darling prize, filched from her husband's lap.
That has to be enough, if but she marks our date
With a stone that's whiter than white.

This is all I can compose for you, dear friend,
Tripping tribute for countless kindnesses.
Thus may your name never be tinged with rust,
Today, tomorrow and tomorrow's morrows .
May the gods grant as many blessings as Themis
Rendered the pious in the olden days.
Be happy, both of you, you and your love,
In the house where once we revelled, the lady and I.
Likewise the man who introduced us, Allius,
The one from whom our blessings flowed,
And she, dearest to me of all the world
The light whose sweetness lends life to mine."

I was in no mood to return to Bithynia and the repetitious company of the honest governor's entourage, the need to dissimulate. Solitude made it seem that what had happened could stay secret. It diverted me to appear to the locals I crossed to be Roman enough to merit deference, if not envy. Spiritual *charcutier*, I laced my anguish in metre:

> "*Many frontiers have I crossed, and many oceans,*
> *To this grim ceremony, brother, for the dead.*
> *This is the final honour I can render:*
> *Pointless verbiage on voiceless ashes spent.*
> Quandoquidem, *chance has filched you from me,*
> *Hapless brother, unceremonially done for,*
> *Tribute here I pay, in due ancestral form,*
> *Take it, drenched with fraternal tears,*
> *Yes, forever, brother, and forever farewell.*"

The more despair mounted in me the less precise its source. Which possessed me more: my brother's death or dread of what I should find when I returned to Rome? Did the loss of Manlius come – the gods forgive me for even thinking as much – conveniently? What no one could chide me for, myself included, was weeping at the memory of those days when Manlius and I teased Solonaki, now as lonely, it seemed, as I, into frowning pleasure chastising us. The serenity of Sirmio's summer days, their vivid loss was cruel comfort, something certain, although eclipsed, against what might or might not be true of Lesbia. Remembered kisses brought more punishment than consolation; thus more pleasure. How much amusement had Manlius Torquatus – his name twisted in absurd complicity with my brother's – found in what he wrote, how truthful and how heartless was it? Did he use the pain he caused me to ease the pain he felt about whatever her name was? Writing makes distinct what the writer without his stylus scarce distinguishes.

> "*Did a lioness spawn you in the mountains of death,*
> *Scylla bark you from her bitch's womb,*

That you can be so cruel, so cynical,
Sniffing at my raw, my pitiful despair,
Heart more savage than the king of beasts?
Numb, I ask you. Yearning for the answer No."

I walked the beach below grassed over Troy, played *xanthos* Menelaus, there to reclaim the woman who had told the world she wanted him no more, his loud war-cry bawling vanity. All those men despatched to darkness, fought, killed, died to serve or confound a loud-mouthed cuckold out to retrieve a peerless bitch. Zeus himself wished that Troy might live, his wishing powerless against the power that bore no name but fate, necessity, later logic. I did not choose to be Menelaus, wigged in hair the colour of Caelius's, never mine. I set myself to rehearse how I should have to be, if I ever set foot again in Rome. I forced forgiving smiles, to him to her, a show of indifference the best revenge. My tears were for Manlius, were they not?

"*Exhausted, yes, by grief, Hortalus, dismissed*
From service to the muses' chaste exigences,
No fresh line can I produce to honour their caress,
My mind in turmoil on a sea of troubles.
Barren since the day when Lethe's gurgle
Blanched my brother's foot with its fell drops.
In Trojan earth on the Hellespont's verge
Snatched away, from our sight effaced.
Never again am I to hear your voice,
See your face? Dearer to me than life,
My brother, sad elegies forever shall I sing,
As Procne, now nightingale, in Daulian shade
Trills for the dear son, Itys, she slew.
In grief as cruel, Hortalus, for you
I squeeze out these verses by Callimachus
Rendered to please you. Never think
Your words breeze-shredded, haplessly diffused,

Small token this, like an apple, token of love
Sent to some pretty bride-to-be, poor thing
Who treasures it, secret, under chiffon folds,
Then when her mother comes, up she jumps,
And out it pops and and rolls along,
Rueful cheeks all rosy with dismay."

When Memmius's year as governor came to an end, he thanked his poets and prosaic deputies, like a proper gentleman, for their attendance on him, but distributed no bounty, extracted nothing more from the Bithynians than puzzled gratitude, step-sister of contempt: what colonial can understand, or respect, a conqueror who fails to take advantage?

The tax-collectors went home with nothing but their legal due. Unrewarded faces promised that Memmius would face charges of furtive peculation. Those whose profits he had abbreviated knew from experience that, while upright governors might gain mild credit from senatorial peers, such kudos won no exemption from prosecution by vindictive equites, pedestrian knights, alien to chivalry. If honest governance became a habit, how would Roman society ever enhance its luxury?

Did the benign governor ever think of his near-namesake, Lucius Mummius, who – four generations earlier – conquered Hellas for Rome, put down Corinthian resistance in so draconian a style that the city itself was said to be levelled, its treasures toted to Rome, models for artisans, trophies for toffs, plenty to go round and be paraded in the Triumph that rewarded Mummius' sumptuous ruthlessness? Corinth was too well sited not to rise again; its bossy acropolis and sentinel plain attracted a swarm of immigrants who quite soon restored the city to prosperity and made it the centre for erotic pilgrimage. Men came to count themselves lucky to get there: "Non cuivis homini contingit adire Corinthum". [Not any old Tom or dick has the luck to get to Corinth]
Memmius and his staff took ship for Italy. Gaius Valerius waved

them goodbye, urged Gaius Helvius to get his enviable Zmyrna to the copyists (he would need a brigade of scribblers) so that he might be famous by the time Catullus was there to mount the best proof of its quality, a scowling eulogy. Helvius guessed that some local doxy had leavened his friend's spirits. Lesbia, he assumed, had lost her compulsive lustre under Asian skies. Did he believe it when Gaius Valerius said he would use his penitential chastity to resume work on that unfinished, no more than plotted, show-piece, proof of unscarred imagination?

> "In days of yore, they say, when pines could skim,
> Through Neptune's crystal realm keels did swim
> To Phasis' waters, lord Aetes' land.
> Those pines, on Pelion reared, bearing a band
> Of noble youth, heart and flower of Greece,
> To Colchis, there to filch the golden fleece.
> On sailed the intrepid crew, with grace and ease
> Swept with firwood oars the darkling seas..."

How was he when he was, as he said he wished to be, alone? Was he postponing his return to face faces which would take pleasure in greeting his expression in whatever light, spiteful or friendly? Did he take refuge in what he pretended he wanted to do, camouflage in archaic courtesies, poetic industry?

> "Athene, lady of citadels, her aid
> Had lent, meshed pines together, Argo made,
> She coached the unskilled bark, its lofty prow,
> Through Amphitrite's stormy realm to plough.
> The water, churned by oars to foam, turned white;
> When sea-nymphs raised their heads to see the sight
> And wonder as the monster passed them by,
> The sailors gazed at them with mortal eye
> To see, but once, those Nereids basking there,

Parading milky breasts, their bodies bare
Against the whitening spume. Then Peleus saw
Fair Thetis; Thetis – filled with matching awe –
Her Peleus spied, and loved. Lord Neptune said:
'So be it! Mortal and immortal, wed!'"

To furnish blithe imposture, did Gaius Valerius resume where he had once broken off and find, to his surprise (or not) that the Muse was impatient? And suggestive? Expecting sterile loneliness, did facility mock his dolorous other self with sunny fluency? How often does a poet presume that he will never be more at liberty than when he sheds the shackle of sociable personality? Then comes the shock of the bare self.

"You heroes, born in enviable times,
Offspring of gods, noble mothers, my lines
Salute you, I often have, often will, greet
You every one, heap honours at your feet.
First proud Peleus, to Thessaly's mainstay
Did not the sire of the gods, Jove himself, yield way,
Concede his love to you, When Thetis came,
Fairest of Nereids, to embrace you? Your fame
Won you union with Tethys' grand-daughter
And old Ocean's too, who girdles earth with water."

How exhilarated was Gaius Valerius as he wove the lengthening tapestry that suffocated personal feelings in its embroidery? Calliope, unlike sister Thalia, offered reprieve from sentiment. Intricate narrative, reproduction furniture of mythology, brought ease from cruel questions, wincing answers. Ariadne's pictured pains needed no modern dress to double for exquisite.

"No more waiting now, the longed for day has dawned,
The palace throngs with guests, all Thessaly
Is here; rejoicing fills the courts, each face

With pleasure glows. Scyros void, Phthiotic
Tempe desert, Crannon's houses, Larissa's
Battlements unmanned. On Pharsalus all converge;
Crammed to the rooftops Pharsalus buzzes.
In idle fields, draught oxen necks grow slack;
No bent rake clears weeds from huddled vines;
No bullock slices slabby ground with slanted blade,
No scythe thins foliage from overgrown trees,
Corroding rust creeps over useless ploughs..."

I promised Helvius that I should welcome being relieved of his scribbling shadow when I was working. On the dockside, I waved goodbye to him and other members of Memmius' staff as they slid away, quite as if, for all my farewell courtesy, I was not sorry to be quit of them. Then, with no witness but myself, I regretted my desertion. For want of companions, I sought solace in the assumed character of my original self. Son of a mercantile speculator, I hired a small boat, double of the *phaselus* Manlius and I used to sail on lake Garda, and a crew of two, man and boy, Milon and Zeno. I learned to mimic their *koine* dialect, the clipped Mytilenaean phrasing, put it on like a vocal costume. Lesbos offered no hint of Lesbia; little Sapphos scowled and giggled, none inspired. Spring's boreal breeze carried us along the Asian coast to the Cyclades, islands my brother and I played at visiting during those adolescent gyrations on lake Garda. Was I seeking a trigger for pious tears, which did not come, or hoping to find a world elsewhere, another, tougher Odyssean self to go with it?

Godless Delos I avoided, where my father had traded human booty, the legions' dividend after Mithridates' bloody effort to fit himself with Alexander's crown. I landed on Paros, harbour a smile of tooth-white *spitia,* quite as if Archilochus, snarling darling of the Muses to whom Delphi insisted he was dear, might have left some thorny marker there for my discovery. I walked up and down the island, was shown what some goatherd told me was the poet's tomb; it lacked the garrison wasps that legend demanded. Paros denied me parity with my scowling model. For exercise, I glossed his acid farewell to Neobule after her father Lycambes revoked the bastard poet's betrothal to her. Archilochus took pleasure in her eclipse, flaunted the replacement:

"...a beautiful, tender young piece.
Nothing, believe me, wrong with her;
And there for the taking.

Under the lintel, through the soft gate,
Don't don't me when I'm on course
Through virgin heat.
Get one thing straight:
Neobule, anyone can have her,
Yesterday's bait, that girlish charm
Ain't girlish any more.

So said I and bedded my fresh darling
In blossoming flowers, soft cloak
For coverlet, neck in the crook
Of my arm...she caught her breath
Like a fawn surprised...as I, light-handed
Fondled breasts, budding charmer,
Encircled ready beauty's beauty,
Let her have it, my milked manliness,
Golden hair knotted in tight arrest."

How comforting imposture, the play that I was free to do as I pleased; and pleased to do it! We, my rented shipmates and I, ate lobster on Nios, its battlement-turbaned village set back from the narrow-mouthed lagoon where nomad pirates were liable to shelter when the wind changed, Neptune's white-maned horses reared and kicked. *Xenoi* were welcome, a lame local told us, as long as they ate and drank at the tavern on the pumice-laden beach. The better the fare, the more time the villagers had to barricade their narrow gates, drive goats and their few sheep to distant, higher ground among the bee-hives on the southern steeps. Yorgo, lame and toothless donkey-man, promised he knew where Homer was buried up there. "Homer the poet?" "The one and only, who conquered Troy and saved Medea from the Minotaur."

Homer's tomb amounted to no more than a rounded boss among the buzz of Nios's famous (so Yorgo told me) bees. Their busy selection of pollen, from a palette of wild shrubs on the hulking shoulders overlooking the channel leading to Amorgos and Pholegandros, gave the island's honey its thick tang. On the way back to the harbour, we met a handsome man scarfed with a few-days-old calf. He took the flower from behind his ear, planted it behind mine, then strode on, *moschophoros*.

Like its neighbour to the north, high-backed Sikinnos, Nios was fortunate, made no Melian mark in history, provoked no memorable massacre. Solon, the Athenian *plousios* for whom Solonaki was named, derided Sikinnos' inglorious quietude, but the islanders, there and on Nios, had – in common with the chorus of old Argives in Aeschylus – no appetite to sack a city, insufficient wealth to lure the self-righteous. The islanders whose age-old poets I had taken for friends regarded me, *Romaion tina*, with indifference. The poets themselves seemed to grow cold.

How often did he think of her? And how? Did he revert, at a distance, to the more distant Clodia? Did he think of her, coram se, *in his heart, his dreams, as Lesbia or did he encode her so only in his poems, as if people would still not guess who was intended? Did he pass his days in the Cyclades in inquisitive seclusion, walking the hills where Archilochus raged and ruminated? Were his nights solitary? If so, from choice or squeamishness? If he had any of his father's money still in his pocket, he could have his choice of more or less venal pleasures without, in his own mind, breaching that* amicitia *which wilfulness could render into a sentimental bond without exclusive pledge. Had he not at least somewhat expected that – like a man – she would take pleasure where she chose? Was that part of her charm, that she was willing to promise what she would never deliver?*

The letter from Manlius Torquatus remained at once unsurprising and painful. May he not have guessed, played with, the image of her in anonymous hands, himself masquerading as another, the self-betrayer, the poet's familiar? Did he crave the pain from her guessed at pleasures? Did he toy with torture, secret delight, and then take comfort in brazen arms, each thrust in whatever flesh was in his grasp a promise to madam that she was not forgotten, not forgiven? The lover keeps a woman alive by playing at forgetting her, infidelity allegiance.

Did he also play at deceiving even those nameless casuals who did not care what he was thinking and so make his passades into something rarer than they might guess, or care? He punished paid pieces with pleasures and pains, loving and hating strangers, male or female, as if doing to them what Lesbia herself deserved, or he wished he was doing to her, Juventius.

Each moment of laziness, each hike along the temple-humped back of Naxos, was shaded with a show of indifference at whatever might be happening in Rome. He schooled himself in Greek duplicity, smiles that stayed buttoned, garrulity in which nothing truthful needed to be said. The impostor played the Greek well enough to become his own cicerone, recalled Solonaki's lift of the negative chin, roll of eyes that doubled denial with imprecation, happiness deprivation, liberty bondage: free as he wished, he would lose his truest self if he lost access to the pain she alone could trigger.

The poet's brain stood clear of the morass of sentiments and their denial, each necessary to the other, garnish of his reveries. When he chose to resume composition, even as he told himself that he lacked the will or the wish, new verses arranged themselves, dared him not to spruce their prolixity, sing their marching song. Despite himself, unless it was a fit, he saw himself as Ariadne, or was she Clodia Metelli, he Theseus?

> *"….Ariadne stands on Naxos,*
> *Staring out to sea as Theseus sails away.*
> *Poor girl, half-demented cannot believe*
> *As if she's woken from a nightmare*
> *To find herself on a deserted beach.*
> *Theseus has put her away, bent to his oars*

Scattering promises to the winds.
Ariadne poses there on the seaweed shore
Straining after him with tear-filled eyes,
Bacchant lapped in stone, while tides
Of misery ebb and flow, mocking the sea,
Fair hair loose, without the fine-spun scarf;

The filmy dress, the broderie that banded
Milky breasts, slide with a shrug from her body,
Lie at her feet, sops for the salty sea.
No elegant niceties now, her heart
Her tortured soul are fixed on Theseus.
Poveretta! *Venus drove her crazy,*
Sowed tares in her heart like thorns.
Fateful moment Theseus the corsair
Set sail from the hooked shore of Piraeus,
Bent for Crete and the barbarian's realm.

It all began, they say, with a cruel plague
That forced the Athenians to pay the price
For killing Androgeos: every year
They had to pick the choicest boys, ripest girls,
Forage for the Cretan Minotaur.
Athens was small; the loss its annual grief.
So Theseus, to save the people dear to him,
Volunteered to serve as sacrifice,
Make this freight of morts sans sépulture *the last*
To sail from Athens' shore to cruel Crete.
Sail wide spread, wind behind him, he made way
To mighty Minos and his palatial pride.

He, as soon as princess Ariadne saw him,
Dazzled the virgin, pure bloom in sweet-scented
Solitary bed by loving mother tended

Like myrtle, by Eurotas' streams, by gentle breezes
Teased, springs into multi-coloured flower.
Eyes flaring, she could not look away,
Fire consumed the deepest marrow of her bones.
O Cupid, what passions you excite,
Joy and anguish in the same cup brew!
And you, Venus, queen of Golgi, leafy Idalium,
The girl is all afire, you toss her
On tides of passion, languishing sighs
For that fair stranger, love and fear
In her fainting heart, paler than gold
She turned at Theseus's rage to fight
The Minotaur. Death or eternal fame the prize.
Her prayers rose to the gods above,
Muttered promises that by the gods are met:
As in the Taurus hills oak trees,
Resin-oozing conifers are by greedy whirlwinds
Ripped up and fall, contorted roots
Dislocated, toppling whatever's in their path,
So Theseus felled the monstrous Minotaur
As it tossed its horns, gored the empty winds,
Then retraced wary steps in glory robed,
Threaded his way back through twists and turns
For fear the Labyrinth might yet amaze him.

Should I digress yet more, tell how she turned
From her father's face, sister's and mother's embrace,
Abandoned her in tears for a daughter lost,
Exchanged them for sweet love of Theseus?
Will you hear of her voyage to Dia's foaming shore,
And how, when her eyes had yielded to sleep,
The man she took for husband slipped away,
His thoughts elsewhere? She wept, we're told,
Delirious, with fevered heart, she raved;

Distraught, she scaled beetling peaks
To scan the wide sea's pulsing emptiness,
Then down to scramble into butting waves,
Flimsy skirt hitched from naked thighs,
And these final sorry words declared
With chattering sobs, face all tears:
Theseus, Theseus, you tore me
From my father's altars, left me
Here on this deserted shore, pledge forgotten,
You said for home..."

When a Rhodian ship on the way home put in at Naxos, I took passage with as little regret as Theseus when he raised those unchanged black sails, headed for Phalera. His father, king Aegeus, high on Sounion's cliff, took the black for mourning, assumed his son the Minotaur's meat, threw himself into the sea his drowning baptised Aegean. Undead Theseus succeeded to the throne his father's death vacated.

We sailed past Nios' slabby cliffs, bent south below the half-moon of roasted rock, skirted the crater of salt soup where Thira's secret heat still simmered. When the wind veered north-west, the Meltemi cuffed the heaving Aegean into fractious froth. The captain pledged a sheep to Poseidon as we rode the bucking storm. At last, we were slipping past the disjointed Colossus, anchoring in the haven of Rhodes. Thumping fragments of the once towering statue stimulated the imagination to restore what might well have seemed merely gigantic if still intact.

I was tugged by a persistent small boy to see the Satyr of Protogenes. The artist had depicted a partridge so lifelike at the top of a painted column that it was taken for the real thing by live partidges who fouled the work by way of homage. Protogenes blanked out the painted bird, which probably became more lifelike in the guide's retelling than it ever was in fact. My own verses were born to copious life from wilful imposture. Playing Ariadne, I dragged out her fury in calm elaboration. Sprung from my own postponed feelings, I was more easily another than myself.

"...cargo a full hold of treachery,
Nothing to stop you, no mercy, pity left for me.
This ending was not the happy one you promised,
Soft words honeying my eager ears,
Marriage! Promise written on the wind!
From now on, let every woman learn from me;
No man who swears will ever keep his word.
As long as men want something from you,
Want it desperately, they will promise worlds;
Desire satisfied, they go, and never call it
Treachery. Oh Theseus caught in the whirl-
-wind of death. I saved you, killed
My brother Minotaur for you,
And you deserted me..."

The riled passion I put in Ariadne's mouth licensed me to play the part on Rhodos. I thought of Lesbia, while I was writing and writing, as if she had been ill-used; I was purged of her, by being her. Had she not led me through the maze of Roman society? Had I not tricked her into my promotion as an object of envy? I had no heroic, black-sailed place in Metellus Celer's death, but... The adversative's falsehood furnished the illusion that I was freed of what had been desirable only as long as I was bound to her, deceit tighter than marriage, *amicitia* its mask. Islanded in a sea of words, I was triumphant, I chose to think, ready to start again, a man. Dare I confess that even Manlius's death was a furtive liberation: my brother a witness gone, who knew me for what I was, and no more chose to be? No sooner had I admitted this to myself, spy reporting on his mark, than I guessed, without truly feeling, my mother's anguish and knew what I should do. I boarded a ship that had called in at Rhodos on its way from Alexandria with grain for Ravenna, city of islands, easy harbour, two days' ride from Verona.

"Of every place that's all but an island, Sirmio,
Of all islands too, the pick, the peach,

As many as Neptune bitter, Neptune sweet
Holds out on brimming lake or flowing sea,
How I've longed for you, and how! Glad to see you?
Time out, for believing my eyes.
Goodbye to B. awful Bithynia,
All those B – thynian marches. Me. You. Here.
Safe! What's more heaven than this?
Done with doing one's duty, wit shucks
Its uniform. We're quit of diplomatic
Baggage, and home, by God, we're come.
Oh lucky stars, to nod off in a bed that fits!
Beat that for services rendered.
How goes it with you, pretty little Sirmio?
Where's a smile for a smiling master?
And what can you do, lake of Lydian hue?
Waves of laughter. Home again! Cackle away!"

My mother smiled a tear or two at my salute to Sirmio. I said nothing of Manlius, but my arm around her promised that I shared her pain; and hid that I knew it distinct from mine. Solonaki had died, she told me; and then her tears were for me, and for those days. I went and sat under the thicker trees where Manlius and I earned our stripes from the old Sicilian. I waited for tears as one might for old friends, but I was thinking, dry, about Rome, never friends.

I announced myself back in Italy by soft means. After I had conned a set of poems which had been sent to where their author took me to have retreated, I fired off the following, quite as if I were my old self, which I was, but older:

"To that fine spirit and fellow poet,
To Caecilius, papyrus, pray post,
Bid him skip the walls of Novum Comum,
Say farewell to his Larian Lake,
Report to Verona. Criticism time:

Serious thoughts from a mutual friend
If he's got any sense, he'll be on his way.
What's this? A smashing girl's charms
To magic him out of leaving,
A thousand arms around his neck
Begging please, please don't go?
So it's true then, is it, frustration
Aflame since she saw the work in hand?
Dindymi dominam…she caught fire
From the heat in the poem, burning
Inside ever since? No criticism, darling;
Your responses keener than Sappho's muse.
This ode of Caecilius's, Magna Mater,
It's exquisite, not perfectly finished."

A woman came, a basket of laundry canted on her thick hip, and leaned to dress the fatter, bent bushes in clean, wet clothes, Melissa. Both calloused heels on the ground, she did not reach upwards, as she had however long ago it was. I rehearsed the cool I meant to take with me into that house on the Janiculum. She looked at me, Melissa, as she turned away. Tact or what – embarrassment, Rome, age? – insisted I say nothing. Was it her small conceit to exact no recognition, declare no claim? Should I have asked my father to give her freedom? Where would she have gone, home to where, who had no home but Sirmio? Her bondage was freer, I told myself, than my freedom.

I dreaded Rome, and had to go there, dawdled (no, I did not ride into Verona, one appointment with grief I did not care to keep) and yet I could not wait, settle for what seemed so easy, so painless. Father was old ladyish, under a draped quilt. He held my hand when I came to say goodbye and had to play man enough to wish me well in what Julius (he no longer favoured my father by claiming his hospitality) had called the shitty of shitties. I soon had something ready for him:

"Who can stand and look at it?
Who can look and stand it?
A rooting porker perhaps,
And a dicey one at that.
Unspoiled Gallia despoiled,
Distant Britannia poached!
Shagged out Rome, can you stick it?
Look, he's always on the make,
Going up, going up, from bed to bed.
Elect him cock of the walk, ready
To call him Adonis? O Romulus,
Even in drag, fancy that one, can you?
Rooting hog I call him, dicey one and all.
Was it for this, O generalissimo,
You marched to the westest isle of them all?
Your strategic plan, was it,
A clapped out prick like chummy
Should piss away your millions?
Unusual waste of funds! Hasn't he
Got through enough, this way and that?
Have you watched him guzzle?
Primo piato, his old man's goodies,
Next case, prime cuts from the Pontic wars,
En suite, fruits of the golden Tagus.
No wonder Britain and Gaul are wobbling
Table jellies! Why in hell do you stand it?
He'd never have gobbled it, grease and all,
Without that proper Roman double-act,
Father and son-in-law, behind him,
Mamurra the name on their scutcheons,
As they pulled the plug on the world."

I did not need to see Caelius or her, my friend or my love, before my veneer of calm melted like the Roman snow my father, Abruzzi-born, rated no snow at all. It took no more than to walk the indifferent streets, wish and not wish to see the people I had known when our secret was my pride, vanity folly. I had little wish to see anyone, but then why did I loiter in public?

"*Friend Varus nabs me down in the Forum,*
Where I'm busy hanging about.
I must come and meet her, he tells me,
Meet who? His latest tart, of course,
Didn't take long to clock that.
Not bad either: nice taste, nice tits,
So far so good; and then we talk,
Talk about this, talk about that,
And the other: Bithynia comes up.
How did I do? How were the pickings?
'Not a soul made a penny I heard of,
Not the heavy, not the light brigade;
Not a palm got greased, not a head
Was patted. No way with H.E. on top.
That bugger was always on top.'
'Rubbish,' they say, 'Bithynian bearers,
You must've have picked up a set!'
What could I do but shoot her the works?
'All right,' quoth I, 'suppose I did have some luck,
And I'm not quite as green as I look.
Eight of them came home with me – eight!
Upstanding lads with good hard backs.'
That was my story; but you know the truth:
I haven't one to my name, not even to porter
A chair leg across the room, and back.
She bought it, of course (easily had)
'O Catullus,' said she, 'be a darling, do,
Let me have a canter, just the East End,
And back!' What's to be done with a girl
Like that? 'Hold it,' says I, 'let me finish.

They're Cinna's, not mine. You know Gaius though:
What's his, what's mine, what's the diff?
I use them as if they were mine, but please
Don't be literal-minded. You had me stick out
My neck, and now I've tripped over my tongue'"

By way of apology to Helvius C., for taking his name in vain, and to announce that I was in town, aware of what was going on, I sent him the following:

"Publication day, Zmyrna by Cinna, my Cinna,
Nine harvests since he began, nine winters too.
Meantime Hortensius is 500,000 lines to the good.
Tummtitty tum tum, tumtitty, tumtitty tum.
Zmyrna will outdo him yet. Selling everywhere!
By Satrachus' sounding stream (local boy makes good)
And as long as ever-ageing time can turn a page.
Volusius' Annals? Dead giveaway. By Padua's bank
Soggy wrapping they'll suppy, for stinking fish.
Your sweet unemphatic line means more to me
Than all Antimachus' swank, the people's choice."

I saw Cicero's Tiro, on some mission, freedman with servile duties, letters to send to Pomponius in Athens perhaps, and saw myself as Marcus T.'s younger other, who returned from elsewhere and found that no one had remarked his absence, took him, if they saw him, as if his yesterdays were but one to them. I said, "How is the Master? Well, I hope." My deferential tone was edged with presumption, as it might never have been before the saviour of his country was banished from his place in it. No one is the same when reinstated.

I was amused by the activity in Tiro's eyes as he strove to match my identity in his private index. In the time it took to smile, incline his head, he came up cleanly with "Well indeed, Gaius Valerius, and will be all the better for your kind inquiry."

Marcus Tullius' recall from exile was thanks to Pompey; fine feathers have their decorative weight. His friend Clodius Aesopus, the biggest star of the Roman theatre, after Roscius' fine profile died, promised that, on the night the senate voted for Cicero's recall, the audience at his performance of Accius' Eurysaces cheered every line which he made sound topical enough to refer to the injustice which had just been revoked. Trust actors and advocates to teach their audience how to be sincere, and – more important – when. Clodia's mentor, and Cicero's, Quintus Roscius Gallus, had had Sulla for a fan and owed social enrolment to his favours. Sulla gone, Roscius became the charmer of those whom his patron had done down. Romans might not forget; they were prone to forgive. The show went on.

At his reappearance, Cicero was hailed by much the same crowd that had jeered him on his way and pillaged his belongings, which were never returned. Lucius Calpurnius Piso, in whose consulate the senate voted for Cicero's recall, was at pains to make it known that his house had nothing worth looting. Beakers marked "Made in Placentia", like Piso himself, he flouted custom by entertaining Greeks to dinner; while generosity crams them five to a couch, their host reserved one all to himself to lounge on. There was wine until there wasn't; he then had his guests shown the door. No one nicked clumsy crockery or nabbed shabby napkins.

Julius, who had done nothing to save Marcus Tullius and as much to bring about his return, greeted him cordially. In Rome, there were no apologies. All were in fee to Fortuna, the bitch. The boni had found themselves in need of an eloquent tongue, if only to flatter them into seeming to be in charge while Julius, Pompeius, Crassus played Cerberus, the Curia their kennel, the republic their shared bone.

The salutes I encountered and returned, as if in equable maturity, restored me to a show of good humour. It was not entirely false. I posted notice to Aurelius and Furius:

"....dear friends,
How about we take a trip together,
As far as India, why not where all land ends
In fretting, foaming sea...
Let's struggle up the Alps, you two and me,
And from the topmost crests look down
On mighty Caesar's monuments, free-
wheel then down along the Rhine and...
Cross bristling waters to Britain, town
By grisly town, my friends, like gallant men
Sample every one. But first – don't frown! –
First pray go see out that bloody bitch
I used to love, tell her from me: that itch
Of hers, good luck with it! Good hunting when
She mounts three hundred Toms and Dicks
At one go, has them fill the niche
That once was mine, and crack their balls for kicks.
I drooped and fell for her, an evening flower,
Cut by a heedless plough, dead in an hour."

I fired that one – reserving the last two, too revealing lines for private cellarage – to the chatty pair, knowing that they would parrot it within the hour to whoever might care to smirk at it. If Lesbia heard it herself, well, who could say what effect it might have? Meanwhile, I schooled myself to be unsurprised, delighted if I could contrive it, should I see Caelius or Lesbia herself, even – such was my resolve, in their absence – if they were together. I relished the prospect of affecting, like a clever gladiator, to be more hurt that I truly was – or should it be less? – the better to put them off their guard. Jealousy too could be a mask, pretence what it was truly was. I was not sufficiently on my guard to be unsurprised by a loud, possessive clap on my back.

"Bet your purse is as empty as when you set out, Veronese. If not more crammed than before with I.O.U.'s to another clutch of those Hellenic iambulators you go padding after."

"And you, Publius, safely downed and outed, do I gather? Our new plebeian Prometheus, fresh flame in his fennel?"

"Corinthian as ever, Gaius V., you and your fancy capitals! Upwards is still downwards. And contrariwise. Your Milesian had it right."

"Ephesian."

"Correct your betters, expect an early grave, clever Catully!"

"Betters?"

"Learn to leave a man with his errors and bide your time. They can have a better use than being too prompt a prick." He held my biceps. "How did you find her?"

"Find whom?"

"My lovely sister."

"Which one?"

"You're boxing clever. Why? The one with her legs around your neck."

"I'm only just back in the city. I haven't got round to seeing her."

"Too busy shooting lines. She's missed you quite conspicuously, Veronese, isn't it?"

I glanced at him oh-faced, as if it were news of no great moment, whatever "conspicuously" meant.

"Hippocleides don't give a shit, that where we are?" Publius's look was almost fond, it seemed: promised nothing, made no threat. Was our Alcibiades taking me to be a hedonist of his own mutable stamp? Or was the assumption mockery in fancy trim? Or both? Cross-dressing was very much his sort of thing. As if under his eyes, although he had already seen someone else he wanted to cosset or needle, I took myself, prisoner and escort, reluctant quick march, to her house. My knock on the door was a double rap of diffident presumption. There was no answer. I walked on in.

She was sitting in a cushioned marble chair in the patio, frowning like a praetor over a papyrus, that long straight back, white neck towards where I came out of the *atrium*. I stood there while she sighed, then smiled at something she was reading. "You took your time." She did not look round, sat frowning at the script in front of her, as if checking whether she had missed some sly point.

"I never got your message," I said.

"I gather you're off to India." Then she did look round and, damn her, denied me the smallest hint of pique or apprehension. She was beautiful and smiling, the double of innocence. "Oh my darling," she said, "I have so *so* much missed you."

"And I you, Calypso, or is it Circe?"

"All the way to the Thynian end of the wedge and you come back with a fresh draught of the same old grekko, isn't it?" Oh that cliquy Clodian enclitic! I wanted to sneer, but I was furiously happy. She said, "Come here, misery."

I said, "Your kisses taste no different."

"Nor yours, my pretty. Would you have it otherwise?"

"It's been a long time."

"Your decision, you bastard. Too long."

"Not to find other company, I trust." I dressed dread with a toothless Anatolian smile.

"Feared to find me drooping in my pot, did you? Or was it hoped? I missed you. I missed it. I missed *us*." She left space for duplication. I elected not to fill it. "You always said that what we were had nothing to do with anyone else and would last whatever happened. *Amicitia* wasn't that our bond?"

"And has it, whatever?"

She laid her hand where she knew she would find my answer, the Clodian squeeze that bestowed junior membership of their Hermetic clan. "Hasn't it? It feels as if it did."

"There's us and there are other people, no matter what, or who, is that what you truly think?"

"Isn't it? Oh," she said, "do you want to have things out? Is that why you haven't been to see me when I know very well you've been back in the city long enough to flaunt all the oriental booty you're so busy counting?"

She seemed to be trying. It aged her.

"Where did you get that from?"

She lifted the papyrus, glanced at it and then, steadily, at me.

> *"Thallus, you very bad fairy,*
> *Softer than a rabbit's furry,*
> *Softer than paté de foie gras,*
> *Limper than an ear-lobe you are;*
> *Boneless as a spider's skein is*
> *Or an old man's mingy penis.*
> *Thallus, a pinching whirlwind*
> *When heaven-sent sloth has a mind*
> *To send wilting witnesses to sleep*
> *And lets you play the thief, you drip.*
> *Send me back that cloak of mine you pinched,*
> *My Saetaban napkins from Spain,*
> *And my Bithynian primitives.*
> *Claim those wogs, do you, as relatives?*
> *Give, sticky fingers, send 'em back*
> *Unless limp wrist and downy flank*
> *Fancy the scoring of my lash.*
> *Yes, nether cheeks can also blush.*
> *You'll jump about like a baby boat*
> *Tossed at sea by a wind...distraught."*

"You're very up to date," I said. "Who gave you that?"

"Was 'distraught' the right word?"

"Nothing wrong with distraught, if it's what I said. Caelius, am I right?"

"You do have that habit. I'm not sure how much good it does you."

"You don't deny it?"

"You went away. Daddy's orders or big opportunity? Neither? Both? I thought of you, often, with a smile."

"And a shrug," I said. "Here's one I haven't published yet."

"Oh dear, he's got his red cap on."

"Rufus, the Red, red-handed! Trust you!
My friend. Trust you I did. And paid the price
In hurt. Aren't you the creep, the red-hot poker
In my guts? Rufus the ripper of everything
I care for most. And you called it friendship,
What we had, you poisonous pest."

"A good one," she said, "to keep to yourself. Were you so very, very loyal and lonely out there?"

"Never so lonely as when a friend wrote and told me what I never wanted to hear."

"Nor so loyal, I suspect."

"Damn you for a clever woman."

"Friends do that," she said, "to displace each other, hoping to become the crooked crutch the sorry choose to lean on. Who was it was in such a hurry to put the shaft in? You do have quite a roster of chums you've roasted in your caustic time. Poor Aurelius Cotta, what did he ever do to you that you should turn on him?"

"It's a wise man who does turn on him. Face to face, I mean. He took it well."

"Those who take it well are often also taking their time to give better than they got. It wasn't one of your best, was it?"

"Now we're getting to it."

"Are we? If it's old cabbage, it'll not be from any wish of mine. I'm glad you're back; and came to see me, even if it wasn't the first thing you did. *Was* glad. Judging from the look on your face, it was ill-advised."

"You took advice?"

She said, "Get used to it. He's not coming home."

"Your heavenly friend treats your house as home now, does he?"

"Caelius? He's moved out of his digs in the block my brother owns and threatening to buy the house next door to me here. Not at my suggestion. Pure swank."

"Swank, yes; pure? Where did he get the scratch?"

138

"Egyptian pay-off, I imagine. You are a sight! Honest Veronese, is that still your chosen part and how honest does it leave you? Celer, I was talking about; and you know it. Rather takes the spice out of the dish, doesn't it, my husband's disappearance? I can please myself now, *sans peur, sans reproche.* You said as much when you were leaving. In quite a hurry, you must admit, if you could be as honest about yourself as you like to be about other people. I wasn't as... enticing when there was nothing to fear."

"I'm not sure it was fear."

"Admit it, or no: what's no longer forbidden loses its tang."

"You've been to Publilius' latest play. No secret who took you."

"I no longer need to have secrets. Another one that isn't one is how much I missed you, especially that wounded pout of yours, so long as I could relieve you of it. Might what really distresses you be that we no longer have to hide what we are to each other?"

Her look knew that I should not long resist her. When we made love those several times, however many they were (five), it was as if nothing had changed; "as if" promised that it had. I was more passionate and she more amazed and – by the sound of it, that double gasp – more delighted than ever before. The long pleasure I took in her was also the measure of what was no longer the same. Pleasure was not joy. Did it matter whether her yeses and her ohs, delight, amazement, were a performance? As we lay there afterwards, gleaming, dread and hope, anger and love revived as one.

She said, "Did you learn that one on your travels?"

"I thought it would please you."

"You thought it would teach me," she said.

"And didn't it? Because you never thought it would."

"It reminded me of when I was a boy and we went to buy that silly bird."

"That died. Something we can never do again."

"Not too often."

"Go in secret with no secret to keep."

"Don't ever do that again," she said.

"Because you enjoyed it?"

"Go away and leave me, that that! Did you cough when you were out there? I bet you didn't."

I said, "I so dreaded seeing you again."

"And now?"

> *"Catullus, Catullus, Catullus,*
> *You're playing the fool; so stop.*
> *What's dead is dead. Now face it.*
> *Once the sun shone full upon you; once.*
> *Her wish your desire; we know, we know.*
> *Wish? Desire? I loved her then, loved*
> *As no woman was ever loved before.*
> *If she was happy, that was happiness.*
> *What you wanted she wanted too.*
> *Yes. Yes, the sun shone full upon you.*
> *Now..."*

"Were you afraid I should have changed? And have I?"

"Yes, damn you. You're more beautiful than ever."

"You had to say. And older, you had not to. And you?"

"Not older," I said, "but wiser."

"Surprisingly so," she said. "So far."

I kissed her eyes and her mouth. She closed the eyes, held her breath. I said, "Why him?"

She opened her eyes as if from a dream; pain, unless it was disappointment, came with the first blink. "You had to ask. And I have to answer: can you think of anyone better?"

"When he's a heartless, cynical, ambitious socialite shit?"

> *"Put her out of your mind. Don't weaken:*
> *Forget! Time to tell her goodbye. That's it.*
> *Catullus seen doing the sensible thing.*
> *Mouth shut, ears deaf. Curtains. Agree?*

Oh she'll be sorry when nobody comes
Wanting to love her. Bitch, bitch!
For the rest of your life, who's going
To bother, tell you how lovely you are?
Whom will you love, who'll want you to?
And what about kisses then?
Whose lips will you bite come the morrow?
Catullus, Catullus, remember: forget!"

"Red? That's putting it nicely. He didn't deceive me for a moment. Or try. Would you have it otherwise? He's also the best company in the world, as long as you don't take him seriously, which I never did. He passed the time, and – like the time – he passed. He's off playing front man for another gyppo scoundrel or other. Money's his only true cupid. Now you're back, I shall probably never hear from him again."

"And shall you mind?"

"If I said no, you'd say I was lying. He doesn't amuse me as you do. He's not so serious. All right: or so funny: occasionally."

"Did he do all the things I did?"

"And more. Now stop it. You'll spoil everything if you hang onto grievances when you know you haven't got one."

"That's what love does."

"That's what greed does, Catullus."

I had to kiss her. "Is what Catullus does."

"It's what he does best. He should stick to it. Otherwise, he's going to sour everything."

"Sour can be truer than sweet."

"Sweet *and* sour, that's the way you like it: allows you to take your pleasure and keep your grievance."

"Pleasure is the sweeter for it, you might say. And I might not deny it."

"You pretended that you hated it that I had a husband. Poor Celer, he suited you perfectly as a rival. He was powerful and gave pleasure the tang you like, but he never truly threatened you at all. You kept us secret so that you could be free when you lost your appetite for me."

"I loved you. I never thought to distinguish between the strands of my feelings."

"Oh what a lawyer you sound!"

"Latin makes advocates of everyone; good and bad."

"The strands were there; admit it or not. You came on like the innocent yokel, but what made you choose to love me, of all the women in Rome?"

"It wasn't a choice. I was warned against you. I warned myself, before I ever saw you. It happened despite myself."

"Warnings can be the best invitations. You prove what you think you're disproving. Where would Marcus Tullius have been without Catiline? Ideal target for an *arriviste* who never made anyone richer and treated the *boni* to lectures they could sleep through with all the complacency he wished on them."

"Do I see the connection?"

"Of course. Catiline gave Marcus T. his chance to play the hero, sport his brave defence of privilege when none opposed it. Hence the patriotism Cato accused him of with his parade – or was it parody? – of praise."

"You've turned into a thinker," I said. "Or are the thoughts not entirely your own?"

"First you make love in a way that seems to promise that you care for me even more than before -"

"Care and desire, rarely sisters. You know very well how close I was...*am* to hating you."

"For not being what I could never have been and still be wanted by a young man who came to Rome to be a nobody, but was cruelly seduced into – what would you say? Something he never wanted? Try it on the Trojans. Whatever it was, it certainly stiffens your rod. You outdid yourself today."

"You're more attractive than ever, you bitch. Despite the grey."

"It's seeing me the bitch that makes me so. Deny it."

"I truly thought..."

"Those who truly think deceive themselves, not other people."

"That bloody Syrian again, am I right? I wanted to think, I *did* think, that we were not going to be like other people. Smile if you like."

"You came looking for a prize that people would envy you and get you talked about."

"Why demean yourself to do whatever you're trying to do to me?"

"Julius was right, you can be too quick for your own good."

"When did he tell you that?"

"He didn't; you did. You know very well. It's what he said when you first met him. I've scarcely talked to the great man, greater and greater all the time. And again: be careful. I'm being particularly nice to you; you have to admit that."

"Implying choice," I said.

"Implying drop the nonsense before it poisons you. And does worse to me."

"Which is what?"

"Bores me."

I left the house not sure who had deceived whom, nor about what exactly.

> "*You long and long for something,*
> *Knowing there's no hope. And it happens.*
> *…I must be the luckiest man alive.*
> *What more could he ask of life?*"

It was true, wasn't it? Then again, again is never the same. I loved her more than before: differently; difference sprang surprises. From certain angles, she was not quite as beautiful as memory preserved (but that silver flash I rather liked). I rejoined my rage, and smiled at it, at the corner of her street. Fresh graffiti placarded the latest loutish lust. As I walked my feelings home, secret, unsheathed talons tore my breast like the fox the Spartan boy concealed under his shirt. Really? Not quite. Similes promise that things are never exactly like each other: there is too much play in them. The Spartan boy died; I was revived.

"Once upon a time it was only Catullus,
Lesbia. You'd've turned down Jove in his place.
I loved you – not as any random Jack his Jill;
Whole families get less than I gave you.
But now, now I know you better, and the brand
Burns deeper, deeper. How come? Don't I know
You're vile, you're cheap? I know. Because:
The more you love a bitch, the greater the hate."

Do words prime feeling or feeling words? The muse danced like
Antiodemis, drew me in her wake.

"Forget what you deserve, from anyone, for anything.
Earn sincere respect? From whom, how and where?
Fat chance! The world's all graceless now.
Long for honest yesterdays, long gone you'll find.
Take me, who hurts me most, and salts the wound?
The man who styles himself 'your one and only friend'."

It flowed like easy blood, my bile, and figured the page, neatly. I
watched myself and felt better for the Archilochan exercise:

"Caelius, my Lesbia and yours, yes, that one,
That Lesbia, the one and only one Catullus loved,
More than himself, more than all his kith and kin.
Now all the roads lead to her, the city's bottleneck,
Glubbing reams of suckers, big-hearted dicks."

Was he ashamed of what appeared under his fist? Did she deserve it?
The Muse is as shameless as imagination chooses to dress her. He wrote
with a hand that dared the poet to deny its freedom and its flow. Those
Veronese veterans primed his lubricity, made him a salacious sailor up
the gonga. The worse he could think of her, the more exciting she
became, to whom nothing and no one did not furnish a certain pleasure.

The hot bitch his fingers mauled was she the Lesbia he loved? Was she not?

"Odi et amo. Quare id faciam fortasse requiris?
Nescio sed fieri sentio et excrucior."

"I hate and I love. Why do that, you may ask? /I do not know, but that's how I feel: nailed through either hand."

Love and hate were also desire and envy. He saw her tireless in the pursuit in which he could never rival her. He coughed and cursed as his line chased her elusive skittishness; wanton appetite her liberty. He saw her again as the slave boy, the licence it granted her and would have given him, had he taken her with the heedlessness he dared not quite achieve, love in the way. The Muse punished him for denying in practice what his stylus had the craven impudence to sketch. She owed no one an account of herself, and did not try to render one, as he did with his measured thrusts.

Romans feared their slaves no less than they petted or punished them; how often did they imagine themselves in similar case? Who did not know how Scipio, even as he posted the advertisement of Rome's indomitable might, while Carthage burned, remarked that pride was fashioning its own fate? Rome's slaves, even as well-treated as the devoted Tiro, might be cherished, patronised, sometimes liberated; they remained omnipresent in their menace. The discounted were as dangerous as they were innumerable. The law that decreed them no better than beasts promised their significance. Freedmen were never free of what they knew of those either side of the boundary they had crossed and which forever striped them.

How often did Gaius Valerius think of Melissa, although he never declared her so, as if she were his truest, untarnished love, whom he never loved at all? Was it his secret pleasure, even with Lesbia, the third time perhaps, that he cast her as the common laundress who popped his innocence: beauty, booty; heads tails?

From the beginning, and before it, Lesbia uncorked a ream of possibilities, whatever she had actually done, nothing compared with what she might have or was accused of having done. Did Gaius V. begin to understand how Marcus Tullius' florid punctuality, as apt for another case as the readiest bull for mounting, while it relied on heaping his prosaic Pelion on an Ossa of superlatives, had little to do with sincerity? From riling reproach to sententious clausulae, figures of speech crowded for an outing to service the Master's eloquent itch. Chickers was neither angry with Catiline nor as afraid as his martial show denied.

Julius was right: the breastplate Tully paraded in the senate house was a brilliant figure of speech, never a preparation for battle. Did it once occur to M.T.C. to think that his effusiveness, when flattering those he came to take as his equals, was part of the endless trial in which he himself, peerless as he might be when it came to rhetorical devices, sought acquittal from those whose endorsement he never ceased to crave, not least when presuming parity with them?

"Don't walk past me, Gaius Valerius. Or are you set on consulting the stars like Julius' sulky rival? She's not worth it."

"How could you?"

"Keep her warm for you? *Pos gar ouk;* as you Alexandrians like to say. She missed you; so did I. So it goes."

"We were friends, Caelius R."

"And are, *pethi mou*! Unless you're determined to put your sissy-Gallic trews back on. I hoped you'd learnt to be a proper Roman after all this time. Let the truth seep in and you'll see I did you a good turn."

"By ruining my life."

"Write that on a wall somewhere, Gaius V., but never sign it. You can do better; and you'd better. She's an old woman, old son. You've had everything from her worth having. Now you're free to tell the truth about her, and yourself, if you dare. And when you do one, honest or no, you're bound to be doing the other. The words'll do the work."

"The truth is…"

"Don't waste it on me. That's scribbling on water."

"You're probably right. Which doesn't make you any less of a shit."

"As Publius would say, common knowledge ain't worth reporting, isn't it? What lover ever gained aught but ridicule by playing the wounded husband's part, especially when he never needed to? You got away with it and now you're not even going to have to honour what you promised to get you there. Dwell on it, if the Muse still has deliveries to make, but let's hear no more of it in public. Meanwhile, doctor C., what do I do about this gout of mine? I can scarcely limp."

"Try a cold bath. I wish you'd done as much –"

"Wouldn'ta cured her hots, sonny boy. Sorry about your brother by the way."

"Launched in folly then, Lesbia, am I. Your fault.
And mine. Wrecked on my own fidelity. The clown.
Worthless, though you play the penitent;
Unforgettable, whatever you bloody do."

"She still loves me."

"And so do I, sorry *signore*; still love you."

"In spite of…"

"Spite is part of your armoury, you and your Parian pal. Deprive you of a grievance, you cease to bristle. You'd be wise to find someone new to wax iambic with. Meanwhile, I've got a new friend who wants to meet you, Titus Annius Milo, out to beat Publius to the consulship, hook or crook his favourite weapons, wants me to jockey his campaign."

"How's Publius going to like that?"

"He's going to hate it, isn't it? And how one Claudian, cloddish as he or she may be, elects to respond is always likely to rub off on the next. No future for anyone in their set who isn't one of them. You could say I was doing it for you, dear Gaius: what clearer way could I have to propose the lady direct her appetites elsewhere? Since she thinks you now hate me, you're free to go back for more, if the same is what appeals to you."

"You and I did not sleep with the same woman."

Caelius pulled me close to him and held me. "That's the wisest thing you've said to date, *pethi mou*. Of course we didn't."

> "*Can the heart ever recover yesterday's delight,*
> *When a man knows he did well and right,*
> *Never broke his solemn word, nor said, "By God, I will,*
> *And then did not, nor men nor gods served ill?*
> *Many then the joys, Catullus, that remain*
> *To cheer your life, from this love's callous pain.*
> *For whatever men can well say, or well can do,*
> *That has been said, that done by you.*
> *Done and said in vain; squandered on a spendthrift heart.*"

Rufus turned to go and I wanted him to stay, where I could see him, perhaps. No, his company was, I could not deny it, like a brother's. He seemed to sense something and turned back to me, a hand on my arm. "Remember what that slick prick Publilius said: A woman loves you or she hates you, ain't no in between." He slid the blade in like a favour, touched my shoulder, went.

> *Why twist again this rack that tears you apart?*
> *Stop. Quit now. Be firm, Catullus. Fly this vile mess.*
> *The gods say no? Damn what they will not bless.*
> *Difficult, is it, to shed so quick so long a love?*
> *Difficult indeed. Ways can and must be thought of.*
> *One hope you have: conquer yourself, the game is won.*
> *Possible? Not possible? It must be done.*
> *Ye gods, call up your pity, shown to men before,*
> *That last reprieve deliver to death's opening door.*
> *See how it is with me and, for pity's sake,*
> *Tear from my soul this pestilence, this snake*
> *That my inmost being coils and paralyses*
> *And to my heart all happiness denies.*

That old prayer I pray no more, that cold heart relent
Or – 'gainst all the odds – she play the penitent.
To be whole, ye gods, I pray, and of this madness free,
For pity's sake, restore my sanity."

I sat for a moment, spent, then I shrugged, pulled the tablet towards me and prepared a squib or two for the company at dinner with Titus Annius.

"What's the story, Jelly-bean? How come
Those rose-bud lips so winter-white,
Morning or afternoon, when out you pop
From bed after a long, hard rest?
Something's up, and rumour swears you suck it,
That fag who makes tents in the bed.
Say no more. Miss Victor's flashing his wares,
Straight from the horse's mouth."

I smiled and went again:

"Friend Gellius was warned: Uncle's a stickler,
Old school: no smut, clean mouth, clean hands.
Gelly didn't want trouble. He made his play
For Auntie, then dealt nunky a hand as well.
Wish, then deed. Silence from uncle. How come?
The old school don't talk with its mouth full."

Poplicola Gellius was quite the toff (his father the family's first-time consul) and used to knock about in the same set with Caelius and Catullus, but he had recently accused Rufus of swindling his stepmother, Polla, and so became ripe for lampoonery at Caelius' table that night. The gossip was that Poppy had popped the lady himself, if only for the exercise.

Lesbia had been more eager with her kisses than I had dared to expect. Those not many days earlier, I had come away relieved and amazed by the revel of our reunion. I had imagined many things, rehearsed all kinds of thrusts, but she had played me, if that was what she did, with delectable assurance. I realised, at my ease, and then uneasily, that what I took for some kind of triumph might as well have been a folly. She had not shed a false tear, told no lie that I could detect, made so candid a case for herself that the furious passion I vented on her seemed to be at her invitation. No potency like hate, love's rough, there had never been a time when we made so free with each other, if never exactly together. I enjoyed her pleasure the more for not sharing it, my own for imposing it on her.

Now, walking home amiably with Milo, who craved my help in ridiculing Publius, his (and Marcus T.'s) loud enemy, I realised that I was yet again yielding, almost gratefully, to whatever Roman of importance, or self-importance, chose to befriend me. I liked Titus A. well enough, his praises more, but Publius seemed to loiter in our wake, with that singular duplicity of his, leering and jeering (close to cheering) at the vacillation which all but aped his own. I could not quite persuade myself to take against him. T.A.M. did himself no great service by intimating, as if to amuse me, that Gellius had boasted of having had a friendly word from Clodia. "Your Clodia, I mean."

> *"Lesbia bitch-bitch-bitches, forever knocking me.*
> *Yet I'm damned if she loves me not. How so?*
> *It's six of her, is how, and half a dozen of me.*
> *I knock her constantly; and if I love her not, I'm done."*

"She has no claim on me, nor I on her," I said. "Fortunately."

As we parted, I walked into swarms of unsleeping demons: did dread kindle hope, hope dread? The best thing, I told myself, would be to find another woman; told myself and did not listen. I made to go to the pot-house where the rough-tradesmen did their raucous ensemble, but veered away, savouring isolation, half in love with anguish. I worked

by lamplight, revising Ariadne, suffering in travesty what I hoped that
she might feel, if I were man enough.

> *"Where can I turn to next? Go home?*
> *The rearing sea lies between us. Turn*
> *To my father? The father I quit to chase*
> *That cruel Athenian, badged with my brother's blood?*
> *A husband then? The husband true*
> *To cherish miseries away? He is gone,*
> *His oars bending to beat the sullen sea..."*

I decided to keep away from her. I should not go to her until she sent
word to me. Even then perhaps I should have them tell her that I was
busy, writing a comedy: what could sound more untroubled? Yet I
could not avoid her street. The first time, I happened (I told myself) to
go that way when set on paying a consolation call on Calvus. Since
Quintilia's death, he was reported to have lost his appetite for
performance, in the courts no less than at private readings. Because he
was slimmer he seemed taller, because balding, wiser. He shook his
whitening head when I proposed his once favourite taverna. I sat with
him in such slumped sympathy with his despair that I left his house in
excellent spirits.

> *"Sexpothouse altogetherboys,*
> *Ninth pillar up from the Brothers,*
> *Woolworth dimeadozen house,*
> *The only slobs with big ones are we?*
> *Lickhairy gangbang all the girls,*
> *Altogether boys all in a row.*
> *Sit-tight assholes bunched up there.*
> *A hundred of you? Two? No sweat:*
> *I'll be right in there among you.*
> *One quickprick allabuggering together,*
> *And badge the house with your testimonials.*

Soppy dicks, the slickquickpricks.
She loved me once, loved and left me,
The girl I loved as nevermore another,
Woman I fought and fought and fought for,
Now she can't resist you all, that the story?
Sexpotluck; come one, come all;
The whole lot come to her in the end,
Even – and it's pitiful, pitiful, isn't it? –
Backstreet bumboys, second class.
Egnatius king of them all, Mr Egg-
face, every madam's top Señorito,
Cunticulous, dentipricks in person.
Si, si, señor, you're in, Dago Number One."

I could not resist going by Lesbia's door as I walked, unhurrying, towards Gaius Helvius's house. I stood on the corner, appraising some pastries which a Mauretanian vendor was toting on a wickerwork tray, strap around his raw neck, figs and raisins in sticky pastry envelopes. I washed my fingers in the corner fountain and when I looked up I saw a man walking away from Clodia's door: Poplicola, unless I was wishing a hurtful identity on a retreating toga. I smiled in any case, as if proved right. I had not intended to call on her, truly I had not; but that splinter of suspicion was also a secret spur. Her door was already ajar. I rapped its dangling knocker in a neat tattoo of presumption. I heard her call out "Tell him to go away," a tearful tremolo in her thinned voice.

"Hullo, Fausta, I just happened to be passing."

Fausta looked at me with as much news posted on her face as she could offer without saying anything. She stayed me with one of her long dark, pink-tipped hands and went back into the house. I took a step or two down the street, quite as if it were a matter of indifference to me whether Lesbia welcomed me or not; but I was alert to the slur of Fausta's feet as she came back and widened the doorway. I looked at her as if I had never had any doubt of my welcome.

"Thank the gods it's you. You're the only person in the world I can bear to see. And I'm not even sure –"

"Yes, you are."

"What did you say to him?"

"Poppy?"

"Poppy? Who's Poppy?"

"Say to whom?" I said.

"Caelius. He's turned totally against me, as if I'd done something to *him*."

"Instead of what?"

"Are you going to be cruel to me too?"

"What did he do exactly?"

"He brought me a little present he called them, some North African pastries he said were especially delicious. Why are you smiling? I know very well. Perhaps you'll stop when I tell you that he was trying to poison me."

"You seem quite lively to me."

"Because I didn't eat them. I gave them to little Dido and she almost die-died. He hates me. You told him, didn't you, how we... did what we did when you first came back?"

"I told no one," I said. "And I never shall."

"I'm afraid to love you again. I don't know whom I can trust, ever."

"We're in similar case," I said.

"Ye gods, even you don't sound like you any more."

The huddle of her body demanded comfort. When I put my arms around her, she looked at me with moist eyes, grateful and suspicious, and sniffed. Lesbia sniffed! Her need made me grateful; and callous: pity dulled desire. Even as I was touched by her distress, I toyed with the idea that she no longer mattered to me as she had. No, she did not. I craved what we had had, but my longing was the measure of unrepealed rage. If I forgave her, she would again become unforgivable.

> "You long and long for something,
> Knowing it hopeless. And then it happens.
> That is happiness indeed. Lesbia
> Is mine, that pleasure with her.

Forget gold. You're back
And I had given up hope.
Your idea, what's more. The sun's full out.
And I the luckiest man alive.
What more could one want from life?"

I smiled, but should have preferred to weep. I told myself that her door was open to me as to no one else; but I did not hasten to it, as I might have, had she been less in need of me. That sniff of hers, apology and accusation in a single snort, stayed with me, warning that whether it was sincere or procured it promised me nothing but demands and reproaches. If she had stayed a bitch, laughed in my face, should I have slept so easy?

A boy of fifteen or sixteen, purpose-laden dark eyes announcing that he might be Tiro's son, came to my house with a message from Marcus Tullius. He would be grateful if I could spare him a moment. How easy to smile when not amused! I went with pleasure.

"My dear young friend, how good of you to find the time!"

"*Cher Maître!*"

"The mastery is all yours, my dear young sir. Your *Peliaco quondam* will last forever. What epyllion was ever more exquisitely stitched? Name one, and I shall beg to differ."

"What can I do for you, sir?"

"I'm a very worried man. Not for my own sake. *Those* worries I keep to myself; everyone knows that. I rather suspect that you must already have been...approached."

"Approached?"

"This is very much between ourselves, of course. By her. Lady Ox-Eyes. Clodia; and her husband, Publius –"

"Brother."

"Brother I should have said. Whatever leads me to make that mistake?"

"On what grounds?"

"You're a friend of Lucius Sempronius, they tell me. Her counsel."

"I know Lucius. We exchange...*arcana, prolegomena,* if you like, a number of us."

"I should be honoured to be admitted to your... intricacies. Excellent young man, a chrysostomous prodigy, as you Atticists might say. And very charming too. Like yourself. Let me tell you candidly what most concerns me..."

"Tell me, sir, and if I can put your mind at rest..."

"You do indeed have that power. I'm conscious of having criticised your work, never – I think you will agree – in the sense of disparaging it, but...well, that is what happens between men of taste whose tastes are not entirely of the same style, even when both are –"

"Poets," I said.

"I hesitated to claim such entitlement, as I never should fail to attribute it in your case. What concerns me in particular just now is the possibility, on account of matters which do not fall within my range of interest nor yet of my knowledge, that you might have heard that a charge of attempted murder, by poisoning, has been brought, on the flimsiest of pretexts and with blatant political malice against someone..."

"Caelius Rufus."

"...whom I have agreed, with the greatest possible pleasure, to defend against a quiver of absurd charges. What I fear – let me come straight to the point – is that..."

"I am going to give evidence against Rufus, with whom, so rumour promises, not without a certain justice, I have scores to settle."

"We poets, Gaius Valerius, we poets have sometimes to endure what men or fortune may throw at us and – dare I say that I set an example when traduced by Publius Clodius? – rise above it."

I looked at him with a face styled to disappoint him. "I don't do rising above, Marcus Tullius." He watched me with, I have to say, admirable indulgence. "Low blows are my preferred weapons."

"So I hear from Poplicola Gellius. I was, I confess, shocked and appalled that such a distinguished man should be so pilloried. I haven't seen the precise terms in which you made cloacal fun of him, but..."

"I can always arrange for copies to come your way, *Maître.*"

"Am I to take it that you've given your word to young Sempronius?"

"I have indeed."

"And can nothing I say, or evidence I show you, get you to change your mind?"

"When I've given my word?"

"I must warn you, my dear friend –"

"You really must not do that, Marcus Tullius. Or I might indeed change my mind. Which would not be at all to your advantage."

"Do I understand you?"

"What I've sworn to my friend Lucius is that under no circumstances will I testify against Caelius to favour the cause of anyone in the world."

"My dear fellow! The greatest, certainly the *cleverest* poet of his generation is also, as I never doubted, a man of superb poise. Your admirable *prise de position* will not, I am sure, be compromised if I tell you what you have doubtless seen for yourself, that this whole insolent confection has been contrived to blight my friend Rufus's new political association with Titus Annius, whose relations with Publius Clodius are indeed...fraught. Can you imagine anything more preposterous than that Caelius should try to poison *anyone?* I appreciate your scruples, but I think you'll agree that we have *la* Quadrantaria where we want her, our – as the plebs have it – two-bit Clytemnestra..."

"Where *you* want her, Marcus Tullius. And now I bid you good evening."

Oh yes, I went to see her again. She listened to me as if she had already heard what I was going to do, or not do. I relished her pain and I loved the smile she affixed to it, the courage that turned a tear into a jewel to catch on the back of my hand. "You are absolutely right," she said. "Caelius knew very well that I never tried to poison him. Therein lay the fun of his accusation."

"Then why did he say it?"

"To please me, to please you, to leave us to each other."

"Did he say so?"

"He has more style than that. Consider the economy of means: with one reckless charge he tells the world that I am free of him, and you that he was doing no more, as you know very well, Veronese, than amusing me and himself, knowing *very* well – oh save the sagging face! – that you would do with some pretty fellow what pretty fellows do, and why not? Now he has resigned in a way that no one can doubt, conceded the bitch to her cruel master. You do want to be cruel, is why you're here, am I right?"

"I have to tell you…"

"This will hurt? I can tell it's meant to."

"I made my peace with Marcus Tullius."

"He'll attribute that to his charm. The mistake of the charmer is never to notice how easy it is to take advantage of him. By doing what?"

"Promising I would not testify against Caelius."

"A promise not worth keeping, since no one would believe you if you did testify. You'd be doing nothing but announcing that he had made a cuckold of you and you couldn't keep it to yourself."

"You admit it then."

"It's what you wanted when you went to Bithynia."

"Feared."

"And went. And found some local Juventius, no doubt. You wanted to teach me something."

"And failed."

"Which was what?"

"That there was something unbreakable between us."

"And now you're here to prove it."

"It's you who're proving whatever there is to prove."

"The love of women is written on water, is that the line? And the love of men in shit, as you were too chaste to say. Caelius is the most generous, wittiest man you're ever likely to know. I hope you see that. And I the most generous woman, to spit on such a man in public, for your sake. I never for a moment imagined he wanted to kill me. You gave Marcus Tullius a present with nothing in its wrapping but your own empty pride."

"We shall see who has anything left to be proud of when the case is done."

"We don't have to wait to see that it's never going to be you, my darling." She wrapped a bow like a kiss around that cold endearment and I had to touch her arm. "You want to see them do to me what you dared not do yourself, the stripes."

"As soon as I think of hurting you, you being hurt, it reminds me that I love you still."

"Tra-la-la," she said. "Are those tears?"

"Thanks to you, damn you, tears that will never dry."

Although almost certainly guilty of bribery and the attempted corruption of Roman officials in the interest of a foreign power, Marcus Caelius Rufus was acquitted of all five charges against him, thanks to the brilliant, crowd-pleasing malice of Cicero's speech in his defence. Its virulence and its wit concentrated on the reputation of the widow Clodia Metelli. By repeating for the public the slip of the tongue which had him call Clodia her brother's "husband", Cicero amused the bystanders, alerted (and scandalised) the jury, paid back old scores. Hatred of the Clodii was fuelled by the shame and temporary ruin which Publius's animosity had brought upon him. If Marcus Tullius had once desired Clodia, it was reprised in sanctimonious opprobrium. She had no voice in the trial which shredded her reputation. Whether or not Caelius turned against her, or she against him, can it conceivably have been that he tried to poison her? Catullus had felt queasy after eating that Mauretanian pasty he bought from the vendor hawking his tray on the Palatine.

I made it my excuse not to go near the trial. It was a fine day and a lazy crowd gathered where the praetor had convened his court, courting the public who wanted to hear Marcus T. doing his cruel, clever stuff. I was not going to go, but went, drifting towards the lazy mass, the surf of their laughter sizzling on the forum floor. I stood a little way away, a crowd of one, heard Marcus T. crack his old jokes to make a new omelette for the people's greed, including the one that made Publius his sister's *marito* and apologised to milk the laughter. I smiled too, in bleak disdain, and was caught as I did so by a glance from Caelius that offered brotherhood. It rendered genuine the false smile I gave him; love and hate twinned in me.

Cicero wove supposition into his fanciful case and had no sense of responsibility to prove what he was delighted to allege. Titus Annius Milo procured a favourable ambience by filling the forum with hired cheers, jeers and muscle. After Caelius was deemed innocent, he found the means and the backers, with Milo's help and Cicero's sponsorship, to run successfully for praetor (whose duties included presiding in court). Clodia Metelli took her notoriety to bed with her. Did Catullus call? Did she care to see him? Did she read neutrality as resignation? How else should she read it? But when exactly, under what circumstances, did Catullus write:

> *"You long and long for something,*
> *Knowing it's hopeless. And then it happens.*
> *That is pleasure indeed. Lesbia*
> *Is mine; and I have that very pleasure.*
> *Forget gold. You're back again*
> *When I had given up hope.*
> *Your idea, what's more. The sun's full out.*
> *I have to be the luckiest man alive.*
> *What else could one want from life?"*

Forthcoming from Holland House Books
in
2020

Selected Short Stories

by

Frederic Raphael